La Morada

A Novel by José M. Valdez

Note for Librarians: A cataloguing record for this book is available from Library and Archives Canada at www.collectionscanada.ca/amicus/index-e.html

Printed in Victoria, BC, Canada.

ISBN: 978-1-4269-0609-1

We at Trafford believe that it is the responsibility of us all, as both individuals and corporations, to make choices that are environmentally and socially sound. You, in turn, are supporting this responsible conduct each time you purchase a Trafford book, or make use of our publishing services. To find out how you are helping, please visit www.trafford.com/responsiblepublishing.html

Our mission is to efficiently provide the world's finest, most comprehensive book publishing service, enabling every author to experience success. To find out how to publish your book, your way, and have it available worldwide, visit us online at www.trafford.com

Trafford rev. 6/22/2009

 www.trafford.com

North America & international
toll-free: 1 888 232 4444 (USA & Canada)
phone: 250 383 6864 ♦ fax: 250 383 6804 ♦ email: info@trafford.com

The United Kingdom & Europe
phone: +44 (0)1865 487 395 ♦ local rate: 0845 230 9601
facsimile: +44 (0)1865 481 507 ♦ email: info.uk@trafford.com

10 9 8 7 6 5 4 3 2 1

ACKNOWLEDGEMENTS

To my son, Enrique, who convinced me to use a word processor instead of my typewriter and proceeded to make one available. To my son, Ruben, who collaborated with the editing mechanism. To Donald Akers, friend, whose patience and experience of such and allied machines made my typing job a little easier.

Lastly, to my daughters and grandchildren who by their relentless urging to know about the following chapters made me feel proud that there were people that cared what I was writing.

DISCLAIMER

The names used in this narrative and the events depicted herein, except what had been corroborated by history, are purely fictional, and any resemblance or similarity to any person is unequivocally coincidental.

LA MORADA

PREFACE

Ever since I learned how to read, I would say at the age of six or seven, while my brother Enrique and I were cloistered in a Salesian boarding school in Mexico City, I would hound my schoolmates to let me read the weekly episodes of serialized books of adventure which they obtained on weekends when their parents would take them home from noon Saturday to Sunday afternoon before 6 PM. Why my brother and I did not or could not go on leave on weekends, and what privileges we gave up to our luck schoolmates in exchange for the privilege of reading the weekly episodes of adventure, would take too long for the present purpose, and perhaps, take me too far afield; so, suffice to say that on one of these stories a Countess Wasilika and her exploits were engraved in my mind, and all my life I kept promising myself that I would write about a sword wielding girl, but which circumstances would necessitate hiding her sex, and forcing her to grow up as a boy in order to enjoy the advantages that young men had that young ladies did not have at the time this narrative took place; that girl, who is one of the central figures, was Luis, as a boy, and Luisa, as a girl, as situations warranted.

Another central figure is Pepe (endearing term for Jose), which moniker is used throughout the story; and Pepe being part Indian faces many vicissitudes and adversity which a conquered race suffered, but which Pepe could not understand and he could not be blamed for finding many situations hard to swallow. In time, through a series of incidents which show not only his mettle but also his discerning mind and quick wits, Pepe overcomes all obstacles which a measure of dignity that his sponsor, Don Carlos, offers him to be a member of his family and the sole heir to his holdings.

The background for this narrative is the Conquest of Mexico, and the initial characters are two first cousins, Don Carlos and Don Felipe, who make their way to the New World and join Don Hernan Cortez and distinguish themselves in every battle, after which, they retire and establish their land grants in a place called 'La Morada' (the purple place). Two other meanings of the title are place of rest, and the color of most of the wild vegetation which dotted the country side.

The wayward element is represented by a pair of brothers with a lesser aristocracy ancestry, who due to their extravagant spending couples with their inclination for the baser forms of pleasure gratification, are forced to look for easy ways to augment their income when their monthly allowances disappear. Their sister, Doña Manuela, eventually marries Don Fernando. Doña Manuela's forte is intrigue which is fueled by envy and greed, but in the end, her tireless machinations bring about her downfall.

One last not that will become obvious is the liberal use that I have made of Spanish and English dictionaries and the usual Thesaurus in order to make as good a presentation as I could. It is my belief that a good reader invariable finds a certain enjoyment in reading passages that are enriched with uncommon vocabulary. Furthermore, that type of person, myself included, unwittingly reveals, most of the time, a penchant for the esoteric when reveling in the use or reading of rich, exquisite and elegant expression.

CONTENTS

1

Description of La Morada, Climate, Agricultural Products, Etc.

In the summer of 1530 La Morada was a region situated about 140 kilometers southwest of Mexico City, on a sort of mesa that in altitude was much lower than the capital of the country of what was then known as New Spain. This difference in altitude gave this part of New Spain a pleasant weather country residence for well-to-do Spanish immigrants, lower echelon noblemen looking to regain wealth and accompaning prestige, soldiers of fortune with very few scruples and some of the higher ranking officers of Hernan Cortés. Being situated on a much lower altitude than the Capital gave this region small but noticeable changes in the overall weather picture during the different seasons, whereas in the Capital the temperature remained constant at around 75-80 degrees F. during the day and about 60 degrees F. to the lower seventies at night time throughout the year. Nobody knew why, where or when this name originated, unless it served to describe the myriad of violets and other similarly colored flowers that dotted uncultivated areas of La Morada. Another interesting meaning of the word morada is abode, a place of rest, and everybody agreed this name suited this part of the country perfectly.

The soil of La Morada was very fertile because it was constantly irrigated either by sporadic rains or showers throughout the year, or by the melting ice and snow from the nearby mountains. Water from these sources replenished the creeks and small rivers that on their way formed lakes and resacas that abounded in fish, and offered comfort to many species of fowl. Some of the more effluent waterways that in some cases served as land marks or even boundaries between land owners, with their limpid and crystalline water afforded clear drinking water, and in the lower banks, fishing, swimming and from time to time, washing of the scant clothing worn by the Indians.

Adding to the comfort, health and wealth of the hacendados, the rich soil contributed such products as maize, tasty tubers which included camote (sweet potatoe) and jicama, numerous wild growing fruits that were unknown to the Spaniards before the Conquest, and different cacti, each endowed with its own qualities. Of this last product, a type of cactus that was called "maguey" gained much popularity among the new settlers because of the high intoxicating quality of its juice. The juice from the maguey plant is obtained by rasping the bottom of the bowl-like structure of the maguey plant. This operation

JOSÉ VALDEZ

causes a thick viscous fluid to ooze out so that after a few days the hot sun will cause the fermentation of the liquid and that results in the high intoxicating quality already mentioned.

It was in this earthly paradise that Don Carlos Monsibais de la Fosa and Don Felipe Mauallay de la Fosa, grantees of "encomiendas", enjoyed leisure, solace and comfort when getting away from the Viceroy's Court in the Capital in order, from time to time, to take more active part in the administration of their extensive holdings; and also looking after the Indians who were integral part of their encomienda. The encomiendas at that time were grants from the Spanish Monarch which empowered grantees to take possession of generous land holdings together with a given number of Indians who were held in benevolent servitude for the purpose of their indoctrination in the benefits of Christianity to the soul and hard, honest work to the body.

Encomienda was the custom instituted by the Spanish Monarch, which apart from the Christian indoctrinating purpose already mentioned, served to reward eligible and deserving subjects with generous tracts of land that afforded grantees a solid foundation for a fair fortune in a few years. In this manner the King did not have to dig into his coffers which needed replenishing frequently because of heavy expenses incurred in the building and maintaining ships and other material necessary to defend against incursions, mostly by British privateers, into established Spanish ports in the New World, and attacks to Spanish merchant ships on the high seas.

Reflecting outlook on their new life, Don Carlos and Don Felipe named their properties Hacienda Cielo Azul and the more significant Estancia Rincon Alegre, respectively.

2

Clouds Gather Over La Morada

The serenity and well being of La Morada began to change noticeably with the arrival of a new type of settlers. This new wave of settlers, on the majority, comprised malcontents who not only did not find the streets of New Spain paved with gold, but thought it beneath their dignity to engage in any line of work; gamblers and opportunists looking to separate unwary inhabitants of La Morada from their hard earned money, and if possible, from their property or any of their belongings by all sorts of wild schemes; and social derelicts who having somehow made their way to the New World, were willing to sell their services at any price, no questions asked. For some time the two elements, the original and the recent arrivals managed to co-exist mainly because the environment supplied to the latter almost all their needs – abundant fruit and vegetables, lots of succulent fish and plentiful wild game. After awhile, rumors began to spread of isolated incidents involving theft of livestock, mugging of settlers or attacks on somebody who having had too much pulque was walking home alone at night. This began to cause some concern and many settlers began to take extra precautions by hiring watchmen and bodyguards whenever the situation demanded such measure. One of these incidents involved Don Carlos Monsibais de la Fosa, a very influential hacendado. It seems that Don Carlos went to what was accepted to be the beginning of the business section of the region for the purpose of hiring an artisan for a job that needed to be done at his estate. No sooner had Don Carlos and his handyman, Martin, dismounted, that they were approached by a gang of four unsavory characters that had been lurking in the vicinity. A couple of deft strokes by Martin with his machete disposed of one of the assailants while Don Carlos hastened the departure from this world of another of the attackers by running him through with his sword; the other two left the scene with noticeable alacrity.

All of the activities of the lawless group were being watched with interest by the two brothers members of one of the principal families in the region, who had the same inclinations, saw an opportunity to wield a certain amount of power by uniting under their guidance the activities of the group.

Teodoro and Doroteo Pantoja were twins, brothers of Doña Manuela Pantoja de la Fosa who was married to Don

Felipe Mauallay de la Fosa, also one of the most influential hacendados of La Morada. The two brothers led a life of dissolution, and by living beyond their means, had run debts that could not be satisfied by their inheritance and rental income. The idea, therefore, of uniting and controlling the lawless element afforded the Twins, as they were known, an opportunity to add to their income by grabbing a percentage of the ill-gotten gains resulting from the information supplied by them, which described the most likeable and with the best chance of success, spots to visit. Most of the group went along with the Twins' offer because it took the guessing out of their trial and error endeavors seeing as how the Twins' familiarity with the properties of the hacendados could best supply all the necessary data for their operations. The sporadic misdemeanors and lesser infractions continued but under some control by the Twins who realized that a regular crime wave would lead to establishment of a regular crime control department which, of course, was considered undesirable by the Twins.

3

Enter Don Carlos and Don Felipe

The narrative of the life and fortunes of Don Carlos and Don Felipe begins in the year 1515. As "Mayorazgos", Don Carlos and Don Felipe had taken control of their respective families and holdings from their aging parents, but the haphazard manner in which they administered their families' holdings, plus their weakness for wine, women and gambling made them realize one fine day that penury would eventually knock at their door. "Mayorazgo" was the Spanish custom of designating the oldest male offspring as absolute heir to all the family's holdings, for in this way the family's name would not suffer detraction of reputation and prestige that would otherwise follow if the property were to be divided among various heirs.

The activities of Don Carlos and Don Felipe not only brought them questionable fame and many encounters on the field of honor, but also frequent unsavory visits from their creditors, for each still held a few plots of land which, however, barely yielded enough income to keep body and soul together.

Don Carlos and Don Felipe were very close to each other as first cousins and kindred souls, and their aims in life, given their difficult situation, were the same – to regain their original family's holdings and prestige. They were about the same age, Don Carlos having been born on December 15, 1486 and Don Felipe on March 21, 1487. Their place of birth was a small community called Montefino, well within the environs of what many years later became Toledo, south of Madrid. The two cousins were sons of two brothers who at one time owned practically all of the land in the region. These two first cousins bore a striking resemblance to each other; and in the overall picture of their wants and aims in life, they differed very little. However, in situations which required quick thinking and decisive action, Don Carlos became the steadying influence, a fact that Don Felipe found irksome at times for he felt that sometimes his course of action was just as acceptable. The few discordant notes in the relations between the companions did not unduly disturb their friendship, but Don Felipe was always hoping for a situation in which his judgment would prove to be the deciding factor for that, in his mind, would make him his cousin's equal.

Having been brought up in a more or less aristocratic atmosphere, their leisure time, when not engaged in activities already mentioned, was dedicated to practice in the use of arms, at which endeavor they soon acquired great proficient and notoriety. As time went on, their fame spread throughout that part of the country so that having no more worlds to conquer, their life became quite boring. This situation, plus the fact their means of livelihood were disappearing rapidly, made them decide to try their fortune in the New World, which action was taken by them by obtaining passage on a ship sailing from Palos June 24, 1517, destined for Cuba where they arrived on August 15, 1517.

At the time of their arrival Cuba was governed by Don Diego Velasquez, a cavalier that by various means had been awarded such an important position in the New World. For awhile the lives of the cousins followed different directions as Don Felipe gained access to the high circles of Governor Diego Velazquez and his friends by becoming friendly with Panfilo Narvaez, a sea captain who was a favorite of the Governor. Don Carlos, on the other hand, from the beginning decided to follow the leadership of Don Hernan Cortés, a soldier of fortune with a reputation of strong character and convictions, an intense love of adventure and an uncommon knowledge of military tactics. Don Carlos was looking for action and Cortés was the man to follow.

As luck would have it, Don Carlos gained the friendship of Don Hernan Cortés when one night while walking past a mesón, a sort of combination inn and restaurant, the swash-buckling noise of sword play attracted him to find out the reason for the encounter, and accompanying shouting and cursing. One quick look made him decide to place his sword on the side of a cavalier who was being beleaguered by four unsavory looking characters bent on relieving the cavalier of whatever article of value. After disposing of two of the malefactors by the cavaliers in the most decisive manner, the other two, although badly wounded, managed to escape through the closest window they could find, leaving the new acquaintances in complete control of the field of combat. The two cavaliers, after exchanging amenities, in the course of their conversation revealed their identity to each other. Don Hernan Cortés and Don Carlos Monsibais de la Fosa, except for a few minor scratches, left the meson relatively unharmed and fast friends.

As time went on and his relationship with Cortes became closer, Don Carlos was put in charge of the outfitting of the stores with special attention given to every type of war material on the ships that Cortés had under his command. Don Carlos gained such expertise from his forebearers who had earned honor, prestige and experience in the latter stages of the "Reconquista", which led to the unification of the realms of Aragon and Castilla that resulted in the creation of the kingdom of Spain, when the respective rulers of Aragon and Castilla, King Fernando and Queen Isabel united their destinies in Holy Matrimony.

4

Cortes Initiates His Quest

On January 9, 1519 the expedition commanded by Hernán Cortés which was made up of 11 ships, 608 men and 18 horses sailed from Cuba and on March 3, 1519 arrived at a point on the eastern coast of Mexico which Cortés named Veracruz. Before arriving at Veracruz, the expedition spent about five weeks skirting the coast from the peninsula of Yucatan, during which time plenty of information was gathered concerning the roads or trails leading to the capital of the Aztecas. Also information was obtained from the Indians encountered on the way to Veracruz about the tribes who were either friends or enemies of the Aztecas, and sources of food and water.

From all data gathered, Cortés decided that topographically, Veracruz seemed to be the best point from which to launch his march toward the capital of the Aztecas. In the campaign the Spaniards were greatly aided by an indian maid named by Cortés, Doña Marina, who having learned sufficient Spanish, served as translator for Cortés in his communication with the various tribes. Doña Marina was a Cacica, a daughter of a Cacique, which meant that she belonged to the ruling class, and as member of aristocracy she was not supposed to engage in housework and other menial tasks; therefore, Cortés treated her in accordance with her position and rank; and was grateful for her help in communicating with the tribes that the Spaniards confronted on their way to Mexico City. Bernal Diaz del Castillo, the foremost chronicler of the Conquest of the Aztec Empire, and who was also one of the Conquistadores, gives us to understand that Doña Marina's businesslike relationship with Don Hernán Cortés eventually ripened into a liaison which resulted in their marriage after the conquest, a fitting epilogue to an interesting and adventurous romance.

Before starting his march toward the capital of the Aztecas, Hernan Cortés, a consummate tactician; solidified his position by cementing his friendship with the Cacique of Cempoala, who before the arrival of Cortés, had held sway over that part of the country, which included Veracruz. As a condition for his friendship, Cortez insisted that the Indians destroy their idols, which the tribe refused to do, whereupon the Spaniards proceeded to destroy the idols and their temples and planted crosses in their place. These actions struck terror and anger in the Cempoalans, who tried to rebel, but were soon put down by the Spaniards who killed a great number of Indians while

JOSÉ VALDEZ

suffering no casualties. This prompted the Cempoala Cacique to accept the conditions set by Cortez, which included that all the Indians be baptized as the beginning of the acceptance of the new religion, which religious ceremony was performed forthwith. Also, as a token of friendship and submission, the Cacique took eight maidens, all daughters of nobility, and offered them to Cortés and his captains; but Cortés, himself, declined such gift, and historian Bernal Diaz del Castillo does not offer a reason for the refusal of Cortés, leaving us to wonder if his close association with his Indian translator, Doña Marina, in part, had anything to do with the decision.

An incident that forced Cortés to accelerate his timetable to march to the capital of the Aztecas was the flight of one of his captains to Cuba to inform Governor Velazquez of what Cortés was doing in Veracruz. To prevent another incident of this type, Cortés ordered the rest of the ships to be burned. The flight of one of the ships to Cuba took place while Cortés and some of his men campaigned for a couple of days pacifying and consolidating that part of the region, where some lesser tribes found out, to their discomfort, that the best course of action in dealing with the Spaniards was to join them and become their allies.

In the meantime, Diego Velazquez set about outfitting 21 ships under the command of Panfilo Narvaez with orders to capture Cortés and bring him in chains to Cuba. No sooner had Narvaez arrived at Veracruz with forces far superior to the ones under Cortés, and established camp for future confrontation with Cortes and his followers, than that night Cortés raided Narvaez's camp and so completely neutralized their power that Panfilo Narvaez and his men had no choice but to accept Hernan Cortés as sole commander.

5

*Reunion of Don Carlos
and Don Felipe
- And Battle of Otumba*

Moctezuma, in the meantime, had been receiving reports about the activities of the Spaniards and how some tribes had been subdued and had accepted alliance with Cortés; and this made him decide to send messengers to Cortés requesting and advising him not to go to the Aztec capital for a number of reasons; but since the messengers had brought gifts wrought of such fine gold as to make the Spaniards realize that a fortune awaited them in Mexico City, Montezuma messengers, instead of dissuading the invaders from marching to the capital, achieved exactly the opposite because from that moment on, all that Cortés and his men desired was to get to the Aztec capital the sooner the better.

JOSÉ VALDEZ

Besides augmenting the forces commanded by Cortés thereby enhancing the probability of conquering the numerous Aztec people, the arrival of Narvaez also brought about the reunion of Don Carlos with his first cousin Don Felipe, who as has been noted before, had been a friend of Narvaez while Don Carlos had been a follower of Hernán Cortés ever since the two cousins had arrived in Cuba. Don Carlos and Don Felipe celebrated their reunion, and as one would expect, the two became inseparable. Soon after a meeting with Cortés, who realized the superior qualities of the two, especially their knowledge of all types of weaponry, both cousins were made captains.

Having been reunited, one would surmise by fate, Don Carlos and Don Felipe distinguished themselves in the battles against the brave Tlazcaltecas, who also were sworn enemies of the Aztecas, the two cavaliers reached their peak of strength, valor and dexterity as they performed heroic deeds in the great battle of Otumba. This battle took place in the Valley of Oaxaca when the Aztecas, under siege by the Spaniards and their Tlaxcaltecan allies, rallied furiously causing the Spaniards and their allies to retreat to the Valley of Oaxaca where they were beset by thousands of Indians from tribes friendly to the Aztecas. As a bit of information, the chronicles number this force of Indians at one hundred thousand. While pursuing the Spaniards and allies, most of the Aztecas opted to remain in their environs to assess their losses, regroup for future action and, to be expected, to celebrate their first success against the invaders. It was at this bloody battle of Otumba, in the Valley of Oaxaca, where Cortés faced what seemed inevitable defeat; but Cortés and his indomitable captains and soldiers, in one desperate but brilliant move, snatched victory from defeat when Cortés and his men counter attacked furiously driving a wedge through thousands of indians toward the chiefs who stood out because of the colorful plumage adorning their heads, and killed them. The slaying of their chiefs caused great confusion among the rank and file Indians and their retreat turned into a rout that resulted in thousands of Indians being slain by the Spaniards and Tlaxcaltecans.

This battle became the turning point in the Conquest of Mexico and is recognized in the annals of warfare as one of the most stupendous and decisive battles that won a war. When word got around of this great victory, many other tribes joined the original Tlaxcaltecans and offered their services to Cortés. With the addition of these new allies, Cortés felt sufficiently strong to tackle the mighty Aztecas again; but this time, with many factors on the side of the Spaniards – well rested soldiers camping around the perimeter of the capital, and this had to act, psychologically, as a constant menace; knowledge obtained from knowledgeable indians about the entire region, and from the Spaniards, themselves, during their retreat to the Valley of Oaxaca; and the absolute belief of the Spaniards' in their cause and in their eventual victory.

JOSÉ VALDEZ

6

Nuptials For Don Carlos And Don Felipe

With the subjugation of the Aztec Empire, most of the immediate territory became pacified and more or less accepted the rule of Cortés. After many difficult and arduous campaigns Don Carlos and Don Felipe, after receiving recompense for their services from the Spanish Crown, and with no more worlds to conquer, and having reached their early forties, the two cousins decided to trade their tumultuous life for a more sedentary one by marrying ladies from the budding society circles of the City of Mexico. They received generous land grants and their usual Encomienda from the Spanish Crown and established their domain in the region known as La Morada, side by side, so that in the event of a merger by the mayorazgos of the two families, or possibly by marriage, the ruler or rulers of such vas holdings could wield great power and influence in the rich country of Nueva España.

On October 7, 1529, Don Carlos married Virginia Bragelone Campoamor, daughter of Don Juan Bragelone Castillo and Blanca Campoamor. Don Juan, a transplanted Frenchman, moved away from the ancestral holdings of the main Bragelone clan, which for more than a century had situated in the environs of the town of Arras in the southern part of France. Virginia inherited her mother's statuesque figure while gaining a little more in height, which gave her a natural air of aristocracy. The fine features of her face, which one could well imagine would vie with each other in their efforts to add grace to her appearance, contributed, as a whole, to present a beauty which attracted many suitors, including Don Felipe, who again lost to his cousin when Virginia chose Don Carlos to be her life's companion.

This last setback was too much for Don Felipe's pride, and out of spite, on November 4, 1529, married Manuela Silva Pantoja, also a leading socialite, that for some reason or other did not care too much for Virginia because she fancied herself at the head of the ladies; circles. This belief came about because she ranked her lineage higher than most ladies of the society, including Virginia, a claim that was not widely accepted. In contrast the Silva family having found the country to their liking, in an easy, unassuming manner were spending their days in happy and blissful serenity, rarely engaging in most social functions. Don Teodoro Silva and his wife Maria Christina who married in their barony, were

JOSÉ VALDEZ

attracted by stories about New Spain, especially the climate which by the way was proving beneficial to Don Teodoro's asthmatic condition. Looking to better their life in the New World, they thought they had found their ideal life, after the marriage of their daughter to Don Felipe; but their dreams were soon dispelled because their twin sons, Teodoro, Jr. and Doroteo, began a life of dissolution and turbulence which made the elder Teodoro and his wife wish they were back in Spain.

After the marriages of Don Carlos and Don Felipe, Manuela's dislike of Virginia played right into Don Felipe's hands when he visualized an opportunity to repay his cousin for the latest setback, and the opportunity presented itself, this time through Virginia, Don Carlos' wife. Realizing her husband's feelings were akin to hers, Manuela saw in the strained relationship between the cousins a very good chance to prosper in her personal campaign against Virginia.

7

Doña Manuela Begins Her Campaign

While feelings of antagonism seemed to thicken the relations of the two families, another sentiment appeared that was to further exacerbate the situation – enviousness. The two cousins saw their goods and holdings prosper although not at the same rate, this discrepancy having a quite simple explanation. Don Carlos and Doña Virginia, except for rare appearances considered 'de rigueur', stayed away from the Viceroy' Court in the Capital, and dedicated themselves to supervising their considerable holdings and encomienda. Empathy, kindness, sense of fairness on the part of Don Carlos and the steadying influence of Doña Virginia's friendly attitude endeared them to their charges who repaid such benevolent treatment with willingness to do their masters' bidding in the best possible manner. On the other hand, Don Felipe, little by little, reverted to the old ways by engaging in the activities that spelled trouble for him in his younger days. Manuela did not object too strongly because she saw that as time went on, Don Felipe became more lax in his duties toward the encomienda, and started to delegate authority haphazardly in order to have more time for drinking and carousing. This situation which Manuela somehow kept under enough control to prevent dire consequences, was to her liking because Don Felipe's strong will, which characterized him during the bloody campaigns in the conquest of New Spain, was slowly disappearing and, by falling under his wife's influence, began to rely entirely on her judgment and decisions. Feeling quite sure of her position, Manuela lost no time in her vindictive campaign against Virginia by gossip, lies and innuendos about Virginia's actions when away from her home visiting family or friends, even hinting strongly about possible extra marital conduct.

All of Manuela's lies and innuendos fell on deaf ears as far as Don Carlos was concerned for he trusted his wife implicitly and Virginia also remained unperturbed because her proud ancestry and upbringing was sufficient to counteract Doña Manuela's attacks. Also, her great love for Don Carlos would never have allowed her to stoop to such reprehensive actions; and for that matter, to even give currency to Manuela's tirades by either listening or trying to defend herself was not in her character. However, for the sake of propriety, and following established rules of conduct, Don Carlos decided to approach his cousin to ask him to try to contain his wife's questionable conduct or to furnish proof of her allegations.

Don Felipe did neither because at the time of confrontation his reasoning powers were impaired by the effect of excessive drinking so that it became very difficult for Don Carlos to carry on an intelligent conversation with his cousin and this, to be expected, further distanced the two families. Manuela continued her actions of hate which grew in size in proportion to the envy and greed that consumed her when she compared Don Carlos' land against her husband's. This state of mind made her complain to all who would listen about an unfairness that had to be corrected; and she threatened to appeal to a high court citing reasons based on the topography of the terrain and the water supply; all of that, according to her, was based on the fact that before, during and after the conquest, Don Felipe had always followed orders of duly elected superiors while Don Carlos had not always done so, while following Don Hernan Cortés.

8

Doña Manela Goes to Court

here were, however, two persons who were ready to listen to her complaints and also willing to do something about it because being Manuela's brothers and always in need of funds to pursue their life of leisure and dissolution, the situation was exactly what they were looking for. On November 16, 1508, the Twins were born, the older of the two being Teodoro, by one hour, according to his father, and was so named to perpetuate the name. As far as the other twin was concerned, who was named Doroteo, with a little imagination, one can see that in a way his name was also Teodoro; and this can be easily explained by repeating Doroteo quickly two or three times; which makes one wonder if whoever was responsible

for using that name did it with a tongue-in-cheek purpose or intention. Manuela and her brothers understood one another perfectly – she knew of their activities and by supplying them with a stipend once in a while, naturally expected them to come to her aid any time she called; and they, in turn, in their long-term planning knew that if Manuela succeeded in whatever she was planning, they would come in for a share of the spoils.

One day, having come to their sister's residence for a quick meal, the Twins and Manuela sat down to discuss the possibility of either controlling all or part of the land belonging to Don Carlos and Doña Virginia, or at least give them a hard time by forcing them to defend their property in the King's Court, an action that all three agreed the thing to do.

As soon as her brothers left, Manuela went to her husband and by clever arguments convinced him to send the King a protest asking him to give his study and Royal consideration to the discrepancy that favored the grant awarded to his cousin Don Carlos, in value, better land and water resources as compared to the grant received by Don Felipe, who had always acted within the King's law, and followed his superiors' orders to the letter form the beginning to the end of the Conquest of New Spain, whereas Don Carlos had on several occasions disregarded and flatly refused to obey the orders of Governor Velazquez in Cuba and Panfilo Narvaez in Veracruz.

Doña Manuela lost no time in putting her plan in action and after recruiting two or three friends as messengers, and preparing a considerable token of homage which she hoped would help influence the King's decision in her husband's favor, she and her brothers held a celebration, for they felt quite sure of success.

Don Felipe's formal protest would have received at least some consideration by the King and his advisors on account of the lavish gifts which accompanied the protest, had not Don Hernan Cortés, Viceroy of New Spain, interceded on behalf of his friend Don Carlos. Don Hernan Cortés, Viceroy of New Spain, happened to be in court because he had been summoned by the King for a report on progress made in New Spain concerning its government, taking care of malcontents, spreading of the Faith throughout the country, including Guatemala and other parts of the south, and last, but not least, looking after the king's interest with renewed vigor because the King's coffers needed replenishing. The condition of this last delicate point, the King went on to explain, was due to the hated English privateers who had intercepted several Spanish ships bearing considerable treasure. Hernan Cortés, the politician, told the King what he wanted to hear, assuring him that income from New Spain would increase with the help of trusted officials and friends among which the name of Don Carlos stood near the top. With such assurances coming from a personage known to keep his word, there could be no doubt whose case would be thrown out of the King's Court, and once more, Don Felipe had lost another to his cousin Don Carlos.

9

The Mayorazco Ploy

The bad news of the King's decision did not deter Manuela, but it made her change her strategy. The new approach was to renew her friendship and her husband's with Don Carlos and Doña Virginia. Of course, she probably did wrong in urging her husband to present the complaint to the King, she explained; but after all, it had no other purpose than to look after her family's interests; and looking into the future, the natural thing to do for any family is to build a patrimony for future heirs, and almost anybody would have done the same under the same circumstances.

The gullible, artless Virginia was taken in by what seemed to her a sincere apology, and Don Carlos, although with gnawing misgivings, accepted the rapprochement effort because he felt sincere affection for his nearest blood relative with whom he had shared happy but sometimes anxious episodes in their early lives, dangerous but exhilarating incidents in their cavalier stage, and finally, their fierce shoulder to shoulder combat during the bloody campaigns in the conquest of New Spain.

In time, all unsavory feelings seemed to have been forgotten and harmony, at least on the surface, reigned in the two households, this situation attesting to the fine work done by Doña Manuela. Lengthy visits on both sides, exchange of gifts on memorable occasions, trips to Mexico City to catch up on the latest news from Spain, attendance at events in the Viceroy's Court which also helped them to catch up on all society gossip worthy of note, tended to cement the happiness and friendship of all. When this level of close relationship was reached, Manuela's time to initiate her new, long-term plan of action also arrived. Basically, the primary purpose of her plan was the perpetuation of the family's name of both Don Carlos and Don Felipe with the entire property of each family to be inherited eventually by the older male offspring, all of this based on the Spanish tradition of the "Mayorazgo". As can be seen, Manuela was going to use this tradition to accomplish her goal in one way or another, and her first step was to discuss with her husband the possibility that one of the two households could find itself without a male heir, in which case possible unification of the two families should be considered; and to this effect, a contract between the two families should be drawn and agreed to, by all concerned.

When Manuela disclosed her idea to her husband he agreed in principal, but raised doubts that any agreement to sign a contract that would prevent a female offspring from inheriting the family's goods and property in the absence of a Mayorazgo would not be accepted by Don Carlos. Manuela then countered with what she thought would be a solution to this obstacle. If the heir is a female and an only offspring, she may inherit the same as a Mayorazgo, but will have to give up her right if she marries, at which time she will receive the customary dowry; and the Mayorazgo of the other family would take steps to effect unification. Further, during her tenure as head of the family she may not dispose of any part of the family's estate, for the tradition is to preserve intact the original holdings. Adding to the foregoing, if there are multiple heirs but no male, the older male of the other family should take steps to effect unification in such a way that the members of the family being taken over, do not lose any of their rights or privileges, or any person goods or property.

When all this was superficially discussed and in a more or less general manner, one more codicil was added at the insistence of Don Carlos and universally accepted and it read that if for any reason a situation arises that makes untenable a good relationship between the two families, either entity may take steps to abrogate the contract by forfeiting the sum of five thousand pesos, which sum will be paid to the passive party within a period of thirty days from the day written notice of abrogation is filed in the La Morada district annals in Mexico City.

Naturally, as long as they lived, Don Carlos, Don Felipe, Doña Virginia and Doña Manuela could not be affected by any part of the contract. After all the points of possible contention seemed to have been ironed out, a meeting was

JOSÉ VALDEZ

proposed during which Don Felipe ably propounded the terms of the contract but Don Carlos advised that for the present he was favoring such arrangement, but he would have to have a few days during which he would make sure his wife understood each and every point of the proposal, for after all, she would be playing a very important role by her willing or unwilling participation.

10

Doña Manuela and Doña Virginia Enceinte – Martin and Juana Enter

Judging by the reaction given to the conditions of the contract by Don Carlos, Doña Manuela was sure of his and Doña Virginia's signatures, in which case the first step of her plan had succeeded. For the time being she would rest on her laurels, and as far as the future was concerned, she was not worrying about nature going against her aims because she never had any intention of complying with the tenets of the contract. Also, if Don Carlos and Doña Virginia happened to have a male heir, she could find ways to take care of that obstacle at the right moment, for having savored initial success, she was not going to let anything deter her.

JOSÉ VALDEZ

While these far-reaching steps were being considered by all, Mother Nature, oblivious to her importance as a major personage in the drama being played, took a significant step of her own by causing Doña Virginia and Doña Manuela to be with child. More deliberation, at least by Don Carlos and Doña Virginia, was spurred by these new developments. At long last Don Carlos and his wife signed the contract that was witnessed by a neighbor of Doña Manuela, and Doctor Enrique Bragelone, Virginia's cousin. All along Don Carlos had a nagging feeling in the back of his mind that he was giving away more than his cousin, but when uneasiness would strongly take hold of his mind, he would rationalize that in the first place, he could take care of any problem with the aid, if necessary, of very powerful friends in the government; and in the second place, was not his cousin bound by the same rules and conditions of the contract? As far as Doña Virginia was concerned, she relied completely in her husband's judgment; and besides, she would tell herself, complete harmony was going to rein in the two families for a long time. Neither Don Carlos, who was sure he knew his cousin well enough, nor artless, unsuspecting Doña Virginia could imagine that Don Felipe or Doña Manuela would have any ulterior motive; and for some time, a good relationship was enjoyed by all parties.

After the documentation covering the new accord between the two families had been signed and sent to the Viceroy, who was none other than Don Hernan Cortés, for his approval and filing in the archives of New Spain, a series of strange happenings were reported to Don Carlos by Martin, one of his overseers. Martin Montero and his wife Juana Leal had gained the respect and confidence of Don Carlos and Doña Virginia by their desire to learn, their willingness to tackle any job and by their unswerving loyalty. Both of them, naturally, were descendants of the last generation of Aztecs that had fought against Cortés; but the rancor and animosity that still existed in some Indians in the encomienda was not part of their nature because only few recollections remained of the turbulent past, and also, they accepted the new way of life because it offered them a life they considered comfortable in comparison to their earlier years. Another factor that probably made it easier for them to accept the new say of life was the fact that although they had accepted Christianity, in their minds they still clung to some superstitions, especially the legend that one of their gods prophesied that from the East bearded white men would come to conquer their race.

Little by little Don Carlos relied on Martin and Doña Virginia on Juana so that she put Juana in charge of the kitchen and her private bedroom. Martin was in a terrestrial heaven because he was made overseer, he was doing the work he loved to do and, best of all, he loved to ride a horse, his own horse, given to him by Don Carlos. As concerned Juana, she ran the kitchen in the best possible manner, and in order to feed the vaqueros, gardeners and other help to get ready for the day's work, she would get up earlier than anybody and in her cheerful manner make everybody enjoy breakfast and feel ready to go out to perform their duties.

After the kitchen and breakfast rooms had cleared, Juana would prepare a tasty breakfast which she insisted on serving Doña Virginia personally for she could only repay her kindness by trying to do everything possible for her comfort.

JOSÉ VALDEZ

These two persons, Martin and Juana, had a lot to do with the smooth operation of the hacienda "Cielo Azul" as Don Carlos preferred to call his place.

While Martin was in many respects the prototype of the Aztec Indian – lean, wiry, of median stature, eyes that narrowed into slits when exercising his intellect to tackle a problem, high cheek bones, almost no hair on his face, with only a few hairs on his upper lip that could hardly pass for a mustache, and his heard covered by jet black, straight and unruly hair, Juana's features departed, ever so slightly from the conventional appearance of the Indian female. Her height seemed to be slightly superior to what the average would be in Indian women, and her weight was evenly distributed and this she confessed to one of her friends, was due to her trying to imitate her mistress in everything including sensible eating.

The foregoing, one would surmise, tended to show that Juana inherited some Spanish blood, obviously the result of mingling of the races, which at that time presented a social condition quite prevalent in some regions where female companionship was practically non-existent. To add a point of interest, one that will show that very few Indian females deserved to be labeled as women of easy virtue, the greater number of liaisons developed into more lasting companionship, eventually resulting in marriage and offspring that to sociologists represented the true "mestizo".

11

Doña Virginia's Discovery

Getting back to Martin who had told Don Carlos of some strange goings on toward the north of the hacienda, at the foot of the mountains but well within the boundary of Don Carlos' property, Martin was asked to explain in more detail about the peculiar incidents, and Martin repeated his story in the following manner. He told Don Carlos that for the past two months, while making his rounds toward the north boundary, he had found diggings of consequence in the ground as if a person or persons had been using mining tools; and on two occasions, from quite a distance he had seen two persons, which he presumed to be Spaniards judging from their apparel; and when he approached them to find out what was going on and why they were trespassing, they rode away in a hurry toward Don Felipe's property as if afraid to be recognized.

Don Carlos promised to take a closer look as soon as convenient because at the moment he had some pressing personal business that needed his attention, but in the meantime, Martin was to do whatever possible, without getting into a dangerous situation, to find out the identity of the mysterious intruders. Don Carlos also told Martin to take some laborers to try to help figure out the reason for the digging around that particular area of the hacienda.

Since everything had become quiet on the family front and Martin had nothing new to report about any more incursions on the northern region, and while Don Carlos was busy at the Capital, Doña Virginia asked Martin to take her to the place which had been the topic of conversation for some time. It was a long hard ride but the effort was satisfying for her because after careful scrutiny she realized that the intruders had found what they had been searching for. She also figured out that if those men had not been scared away, they would have succeeded in covering up their work and tracks, and their actions and purpose would have remained a secret. Doña Virginia kept her counsel to herself and collected some dirt and rocks before undertaking the long, hard ride home. She did not want to inform her husband of her findings until she was sure of what she already suspected; and to this effect, she made plans to consult an expert metallurgist.

Teodoro and Doroteo who were the culprit trespassers, as may have been surmised, had found out that a very rich deposit of silver, almost on the surface of the ground, of expensive proportions, existed on the place where the two brothers had been digging, having themselves found out about it from an old Indian in Don Felipe's encomienda. The twins had refrained from telling their sister or Don Carlos hoping for a reward. But since they guessed that the secret was no longer a secret, they decided to tell their sister who gave them a tongue-lashing, not because what they had done was really wrong but because with their bungling they had done away with a very good chance for her to strike a good deal for that particular piece of land.

In the meantime, Doña Virginia learned from the assayer of the high purity of the samples she had brought and notified her husband, who took the necessary steps to record the finding with the Viceroy's office that took action immediately to send a special messenger with all the appertaining information to the King's Court. As soon as practical the King gave permission to start working the rich deposit from which the King would receive the customary one third. Since quite some time was to elapse before any action could officially be undertaken, taking into consideration crossing of the Atlantic two times, everything seemed to lapse into a sort of status quo, except for Doña Virginia and Doña Manuela who continued making preparations for their addition or additions to their families.

JOSÉ VALDEZ

12

Doña Manuela Retrieves Chestnuts From The Fire

While Doña Virginia and Doña Manuela were awaiting the arrival of their respective blessed event, a feeling of anxiety seemed to take hold on them, although neither showed it on the surface; and it did not have anything special to do with the natural expectancy of childbirth, but on what each birth would disclose, male or female offspring; and that feeling was affecting the two women in a different manner.

To Doña Manuela, having a male child meant that one half of her plan would be accomplished; if not, although she would be disappointed, she had other options – eventually she would come up with a male child; and if nature somehow negated her efforts, her sublime confidence assured her that, given her intellectual nimbleness and her fraudulent nature could at any given time extricate herself out of any predicament so that she could accomplish her goal. A quite different preoccupation engulfed Doña Virginia at times to such an extent that she would become a bundle of nerves, and usually it would take all the solicitous care of Don Carlos to calm her. First of all she would bring up the possibility that her event could very well turn out to be a girl, and Don Carlos would help her dismiss such thought by assuring her that other offspring would follow, and eventually a Mayorazgo would appear. Secondly, although everybody as of the opinion that the contract was for the good of the family and perpetuation of the family name, which by then had become quite well-known and famous, her good common sense prevented her from telling even her husband that her mind was mulling over and over, that perhaps she should have tried to prevail on her husband to reject the agreement. Lastly, and to add to her discomfort, quite often she had presentiment of impending danger; a feeling which was very difficult to shake off no matter how hard Don Carlos tried to allay her fears; and the closer the time of her confinement, the worse she felt.

As was pointed out before, when Teodoro and his twin brother Doroteo went to their sister with the bad news that they were quite sure that Martin knew who they were, and Doña Virginia found out what they had been doing, she was very angry and in no uncertain terms informed them that their action had ruined her plan to buy or lease that piece of land from Don Carlos if necessary, by subterfuge. Now, she added, she had to do something she hated to do, which was to go to Don Carlos and Doña Virginia to try to explain their trespassing and maybe apologize. Just as she figured she had to do, she went to Don Carlos and explained that her brothers had been duped by an old Indian who had told them of an existence of a cavern where lots of gold and jewelry had been stored to keep it away from the Spanish conquerors; and this treasure was guarded by the spirit of an old Aztec warrior. She continued that neither of her brothers believed in spirits, but driven by natural curiosity, they thought it would be worth to see if there really was a cavern; and whatever digging was done had been for the purpose of finding the entrance to the mysterious cavern. Of course, she added, they would have notified Don Carlos if they had discovered anything. Her two brothers meant no harm and besides, Don Carlos had now found a deposit of a precious metal that would enhance his fortune, thanks to the curiosity of her brothers. If Don Carlos and Doña Virginia received Doña Manuela's explanations with a grain of salt, they did not outwardly show it, but in a rather pleasant manner advised Doña Manuela that as soon as all documentation was completed, all concerned would share in this stroke of good luck.

13

The Twins Try Again

Teodoro and Doroteo, in a way, were glad the unhappy episode had been settled and to all purposes practically forgotten by everybody, except by their friends who somehow found out about the ill-fated adventure, and who whenever opportunity presented itself would in an eerie, spectral tone mention ghosts, phantoms, spirits and Aztec warriors; and all would have a good laugh at the expense of the Twins. This taunting made the two brothers very unhappy and at times when they could stand no more the jibing and jeering, they would swear to take vengeance on Martin, Don Carlos and everybody else that would stand in their way. Whoever knew the Twins knew those were not idle threats, and the friends of

JOSÉ VALDEZ

Teodoro and Doroteo knew it better than anyone else. Seeing them in such an ugly mood made the cantina customers slow down on their reference to the incident, and anyway, they had all had enough fun from the adventure of the Twins.

Teodoro and Doroteo did everything together, were practically inseparable, and being at an age when everything seemed easy and feasible, they spent almost all their time with their friends drinking and gambling, which activities depleted their funds, they would start looking for some way to obtain funds to tide them until the next period. Their usual mode of operation would start by outright asking their sister for money, but sometimes she would refuse, for whatever reason. The next move was to apply for loans that with compounded interest would cut deeply into the next month's allowance. These tactics continued until the time came when they would borrow an amount almost equal to nest month's income. The moneylenders, in the meantime, did not press too hard because they knew that the time was not too far off when Teodoro would come into his own as Mayorazgo since the elder Teodoro's asthmatic condition had taken a turn for the worse. Nevertheless, when money had almost disappeared, their only recourse was to drink cheaper liquor, even pulque, and to try to figure how to improve their condition by looking for any other source of income.

It was on one of these occasions that Doroteo came up with the idea of approaching a certain assayer with the proposition of offering some of the high grade silver which they expected to extract surreptitiously from the newly found mine. The assayer, a shady character who had been accused before of many illegal operations but never convicted, was agreeable to their plan because it meant easy money for him also; and as far as the brothers were concerned, they realized they would not get anything close to the true value, but all that mattered to them was to have enough funds until they received their next month's allowance. Since the incident of the discovery of the deposit of silver had been resolved amicably, it was not thought to be necessary to exercise strict vigilance, a condition that was to work perfectly into the plans of the Twins who lost no time in extracting as much of the precious metal as possible.

JOSÉ VALDEZ

14

Pepito's Early Life

Being instrumental in the silver episode incident, Martin was praised for his loyalty and fine performance in his work, and this also made his wife Juana very happy for her husband. Martin and Juana lived a happy life, a little better than the rest of the settlers of the encomienda, and their aims were always to try to do their job in the best manner possible to repay their benefactors for all favors received. There was also another reason which made Martin and Juana that no matter what they did, they would always feel indebted to Don Carlos and Doña Virginia because they were brought together in the encomienda; and having united their destinies according to Christian rite, their union had been blessed by the arrival of Pepito, who at around this time was about four years old.

Pepito was a very bright boy, good looking by any standard and quite precocious. Martin and Juana showered Pepito with great love, and he in turn, repaid them with such endearing love and affection that Martin and Juana, within their means could not find enough things to give him or do for him. Juana would take him to the kitchen and let him help in some ways that made Pepito very happy because he felt that he was doing something useful. Some other times Juana would give Pepito a piece of the first pie or cookies out of the oven, and he would sit in a corner and wait patiently until his mother had some time to spend with him.

As for Martin, after finishing his chores, he would take Pepito for a ride in his horse around the open fields of the hacienda. He showed Pepito the grazing sections of the cattle and horses, the sections where beans, corn and other needed vegetables were planted and raised, the pens where the field hands branded the cattle and trained the horses. There was also the teaching about the wild flowers and herbs, some of which had special curative powers, for example, a species of wild lemon whose small, almost round leaves would cure a headache when applied to the temple on both sides of the head and held there with the aid of a little bit of fat or grease, or even some saliva. There was a shrub that a piece of the stem could allay thirst, and a person could go for hours without the need for water, when the piece of the stem was held in the person's mouth.

Martin would also teach him how to tell poisonous from the non-poisonous, about the wild fruits, which abounded

JOSÉ VALDEZ

everywhere, something that came handy at times. He also would tell Pepito that in time he would probably have his own horse and do the same kind of work, and Pepito would listen with rapture and could hardly wait for that wonderful time to arrive. Along with those teachings Martin would tell his son stories from his experience and also the legends of their past, traditions and origin, all of which Pepito listened, absorbed and deeply impressed in his mind because all that his father told him helped him understand a little bit more of his place of life.

Pepito tried to understand as much as he could, and being quite intelligent, he saw many things that he could not grasp, but he also realized that perhaps in time he would see things more clearly. For the moment he was wondering why he was learning to speak Spanish and not Aztec that his father had talked about; and he reasoned that if learning the language that Don Carlos and Doña Virginia spoke had given them somehow more power and influence, then he would try to this effect, he would try to listen every time Don Carlos and Doña Virginia talked to one another and in that manner he was advancing in his desire to learn as much as he could. All in all, Pepito, even at that age was a model child, and with a mentality of a much older boy.

15

Doña Virginia's Fateful Accident

It is said that some people have the gift of clairvoyance and prophecy, as witness the many instances described in the Good Book; and still others, on a lesser scale, are so sensitive that at times their entire being is engulfed by whatever seems to pervade the atmosphere, and it is said then that a condition of premonition or forewarning exists. It was on a cloudy and dreary day that Doña Virginia awoke with a feeling of uneasiness and apprehension that kept her from enjoying her daily morning bath and tasty breakfast that Juana had prepared for her. A day when she just knew that nothing was going to go right for her, although what could go wrong if she was going to be cooped up in the house on account of her

JOSÉ VALDEZ

condition. She detested the silence that engulfed the house when Juana was not with her because there was the cleaning of the kitchen and the rest of the house, and this day Don Carlos had left early because he wanted the supervising of a new pen and lean-to for the cattle. All in all, she went back to bed to enjoy her misery.

While thinking about what to do, she thought about what Doctor Bragelone had told her to do some walking for exercise and to try to breathe fresh air whenever possible without getting too much humidity and she decided to go for a walk for she thought that would be the best way to exercise and get some fresh air.

When she was ready to go, a quite strange feeling seemed to assail her, a feeling that grew stronger as soon as she left the house. She wanted to go back but she felt that the feeling of uneasiness would go away once she got to the stables where she wanted to see the pretty, gentle mare that she used to ride.

Halfway to the stables again she felt an eerie sensation as if something was trying to stop her, but she shook it off blaming it on the way she had been feeling since she woke up that morning. Continuing on her way, right at the entrance of the main gate, as luck would have it, she stepped on a pitchfork that she did not see because it was hidden by dirt, straw and other dried matter, and she fell forward. Antonio, the stable boy, ran to Doña Virginia's aid when he heard her faint calls for help, but when Antonio got there, Doña Virginia was already half way on her feet and assured Antonio that she was feeling quite well. Doña Virginia started to walk toward the house but half way there she started to feel an acute pain in her abdomen that she barely made it to the main door of the house.

Juana, in the meantime, had seen her leave, and when she saw her return she ran to help her to her bedroom for she realized Doña Virginia's serious condition. While Doña Virginia was lying in bed as comfortable as Juana could arrange it, she told Juana to notify Don Carlos and her cousin, Enrique Bragelone, who had recently arrived from Spain where he had been practicing medicine. In a very short time Don Carlos, Don Enrique and Juana were hovering around Doña Virginia, who seemed a little bit pale but otherwise feeling much better. After a cursory examination, Doctor Bragelone told Don Carlos that he was going to do more tests and a closer examination, and he would like to have Juana's help.

After Don Carlos left the bedroom leaving Doctor Bragelone and Juana to take care of Doña Virginia, and not more than an hour had elapsed, the cries of a baby could be heard all over the house. Don Carlos, who was in the next room waiting to be called, started to have a variety of thoughts – he was a father, was his wife doing well and lastly, was the baby a boy or a girl, date of birth being June 4, 1550.

Things having settled and Juana having been instructed on what to do if Doña Virginia or the baby needed anything out of the ordinary, Doctor Bragelone went to the adjoining bedroom to talk to Don Carlos to assure him that for the present Doña Virginia was resting comfortably even though she had gone through a difficult situation; and the baby, a little girl, was doing very well, also. This last bit of information, although quite unconsciously, gave Don Carlos a start which

JOSÉ VALDEZ

caused the Doctor to ask if anything was wrong. Don Carlos did not give Don Enrique an answer but promised to explain everything as soon as his wife awakened from her restful sleep. While his wife was still resting, Don Carlos entered her bedroom to take a look at his wife and the baby, and to advice Juana that under no circumstances she was to divulge anything about the baby, especially about the baby's sex; in fact, all she was to say, if pressed, was that the baby was a boy. Juana assured Don Carlos that she understood perfectly those instructions, and she was glad to be in a position to do something for Don Carlos and Doña Virginia.

16

The Baby Plays a Dual Role

An hour later, Doña Virginia opened her eyes and her first reaction was to ask for the baby, who had been in Juana's lap practically since birth. Her joy was great at seeing such a beautiful baby, and she and Juana spent several minutes in a discussion of the baby's features, and wondering about a purple birthmark in the form of an "L" on the right side of her neck, an inch and a half or two inches under but past the middle of her right mandible. The birthmark was of a size that could not be detected at first sight, but due to its purplish color and set against the white akin as background it stood out whenever Luisa (the proposed baby's name) turned her head 60 degrees to 70 degrees to the left. The consensus was

JOSÉ VALDEZ

that the birthmark was a small matter, in fact, it served notice to everybody that she was not to be mistaken for anybody else, and also, Juana added, it enhanced Luisa's personality.

It goes without saying that Doña Virginia had already learned about the baby's sex when Don Carlos and Doctor Bragelone walked in. Don Carlos and his wife exchanged glances for an instant, and the mute question was asked and its answer given. For the moment, however, the baby's birth overcame whatever else was in their minds, and they seemed gloriously happy, reveling in the baby's beauty and not expecting, obviously, the tragic news that Doctor Bragelone was about to reveal to them.

Everybody became silent when the doctor announced that he hoped his diagnosis was wrong, but his examination had been thorough and it pained him to tell Don Carlos and Doña Virginia that in his opinion they would never have any more children. He added that the fall had damaged some internal organs to such an extent that Mother Nature could not repair them, and he regretted that he could not either. However, he continued, Doña Virginia was going to regain her good health after a rest of a few days. After the doctor's announcement a dead silence ensued, and after a minute or two a sad scene developed when Doña Virginia burst into uncontrollable weeping and sobbing, Don Carlos talking to his wife trying to console her, and Juana crying and doing her best to pacify the baby who had become uneasy and querulous due to the strange noise pervading in the bedroom.

Due to the fact that Antonio, the stable boy, had seen Doña Virginia fall, the news of the accident spread through the vicinity, and that plus the fact that Doctor Bragelone had been summoned was bound to reach Doña Manuela's ears, who naturally would try to see the baby, for more reasons than one. In order to counteract Doña Manuela's design whatever it would be, Don Carlos made a move that was going to affect the lives of many persons; and to that effect, he took Doctor Bragelone aside and explained at length the far reaching facets of the family agreement, and why he had decided to pass Luisa, as Luis, a boy, as long as possible during which time things would change, or he decided to abrogate the contract.

Doctor Bragelone reminded Don Carlos that he understood the situation perfectly because he had been a witness when the contract had been signed, and assured him that he would not mind giving his word about not divulging the baby's sex. He further told Don Carlos that he would do all he could to help carry out the deceit, even as far as signing the official records with Luis as the baby's name. Doña Virginia, because of her strong character, willed herself into a state of serenity in order to do her part in the scheme, for Doña Manuela was bound to come soon if for nothing else than to try to find out the baby's sex. Also, it was most important that she appear as if she had suffered no ill effects form her fall.

JOSÉ VALDEZ

17

Pepito Goes For A Short Ride

On the third day Doña Manuela came and everything went according to plan. She was shown the baby, but by adroit handling on Juana's part did not succeed in holding the baby thus preventing Doña Manuela's deft fingers from touching certain baby's part that would have revealed its sex. Juana's move in taking Luis from his mother, ostensibly to give him a bath, was seen as a quite natural action which did not arouse any untoward reaction from Doña Manuela who reasoned that there would be plenty of time to find out for sure the information she was anxious to obtain.

Women talk followed during which Manuela congratulated Doña Virginia about Luis, and soon after, took her leave promising to return when she had regained her health completely so that they could take a walk and have a nice visit. Doña Virginia agreed that it would be something nice to look forward to, and each said adios. Having gone through this first encounter, all concerned seemed to acquire a certain amount of confidence that the deception could be carried without any undue difficulty if Juana, who was going to be in charge of Luis most of the time, exercised enough care to keep the baby at arm's length from anybody who showed any interest in the baby's sex. Things went on without any incidence for a few months after which everybody accepted Luis for what he appeared to be.

During the upheaval caused by Doña Virginia's accident and subsequent birth of Luisa, plus the week's rest mandated by Doctor Bragelone, Teodoro and Doroteo, as the saying goes, made hay while the sun shined by extracting as much metal as they could, which brought them enough funds to regain their popularity at their usual haunts. In the meantime, Pepito, too young to understand all that had been going on, knew only that he missed riding with his father who had been instructed by Don Carlos to be in readiness day or night should any medicine be needed, or some messenger service be required for any reason.

Things having returned almost to normal except for the extra care of the baby by Juana, Martin's time was spent taking care of Pepito while Juana was at Doña Virginia's side. It was then that Don Carlos told Martin to resume making his rounds. When Martin told Pepito to get ready to go riding, Pepito was overcome with joy because he loved his father very much and wanted to ride with him with the sun and wind

JOSÉ VALDEZ

on his face, while listening to his father tell him about nature and its creatures, and at other times would sing an old ballad from his boyhood.

On this particular day Martin and Pepito arrived after a couple of hours of slow trot to a clearing that had become known as "El Cesteadero" which means a resting place; and it was well named because of the abundant water from a good sized brook stemming from a main waterway; and the inviting shade from three half-grown "ahuehuete" trees. The limpid water from the stream nurtured water lilies and very thick growth of reeds covered the banks so that anybody, male or female, who wanted to cool could do so unencumbered by clothing and still be protected from prying eyes. Martin and Pepito did exactly that, after unsaddling the horse and removing the bit so that it could graze and rest awhile.

18

Heinous Crime at "El Cesteadero"

After a short dip in the cool water Martin and Pepito were about to lie down under the trees when Martin heard galloping of what he judged to be two riders. Sensing trouble, Martin decided to investigate, but first thinking of about the safety of Pepito, he told his son to hide in the thick reeds and not to come out no matter what he saw or heard. Martin had a good vantage point form where he could see the riders and not be seen by them however, his position was discovered by the interlopers when his own horse gave a sonorous neigh which brought a confrontation between Martin and the two riders. Even if Martin had tried to escape, he would have been caught before getting to his unsaddled horse; and besides, he

JOSÉ VALDEZ

would not have left his son to an unknown fate. Teodoro and Doroteo, who were the riders in question, knew what would be their fate if Martin went back to the hacienda to tell Don Carlos – jail, torture, even the rack, for stealing from the King's property, which was the worst offence imaginable.

Desperate for a solution to their predicament they asked Martin to swear upon the rosary that he carried around his neck that he would not denounce them but Martin refused. Seeing no alternative to their problem they decided to do away with Martin, and attacked him with their swords while Martin tried to defend himself with his machete which he grabbed when he saw that he was going to be attacked. From the beginning Martin knew he was fighting a losing battle. Fighting the two enemies on foot would have been bad enough although with a little bit of luck he could have had a remote chance of survival; but adversaries on horseback could only spell a quick defeat; and to make the situation more desperate, if that could be possible, Martin knew that he could not expect any mercy from the two brothers. Martin fought fiercely, he fought for his Juana, he fought for his patron who had been so kind to him, and lastly, he fought for his pride as the Aztec warrior that he had once been in his early teens when he had dared to go against the invaders. He again felt the excitement, joy and the supreme disregard for death that was staring him in the face, and he again saw that always the edge of battle went to the Spaniards because of their horses. Never had Martin seen the face of horses that close – horses that hated him, horses that despised him because he was puny in comparison, horses that wanted to knock him down and trample him. Of course he had seen the face of a horse that close, but it really was not a horse, that was his friend who, imagination told him, wanted to come to his aid.

Instinctively, Martin withdrew to one of the trees to prevent attack form his rear and stood his ground. For a split second luck seemed to be on his side when one of his lunges knocked the sword from Doroteo's hand, inflicting a serious wound to his forearm. At the same time the sword, on its way to the ground, cut a gash on the left front leg of Doroteo's horse, damaging a tendon and causing horse and horseman to fall in a heap. Martin jumped immediately with the exhilaration of possible victory because he felt sure on a one to one confrontation he could hold his own against Teodoro. In his haste, anxiety and desire to finish one of his foes, one who lay prostrate and defenseless, Martin lost tract for a fatal instant about his other attacker who maneuvered to Martin's right side and ran him through the area of the right lung, the point of the sword emerging at the lower left side of Martin's abdomen since the trajectory of the blade originated from a level dictated by the height of the horse.

Having disposed of what they thought was the only witness, the Twins took care of their wounds as best they could and confronted the problem of a hobbled horse. It was obvious they could not dispose of the animal right then and there; and it was also imperative to leave the scene of the crime as soon as possible because Martin's failure to return would bring unwanted visitors looking for Martin, so Doroteo rode double and both brothers left at a pace to conform with that of a hobbled horse. Martin expired trying to call his son, but blood gushing from his mouth prevented him from telling Pepito the names of his assassins.

19

Pepito's Lonely Walk Home

All through the struggle Pepito had been hiding in a thick clump of reeds and had been watching all that had been taking place, but he never made a sound or uttered a word perhaps the innate instinct of self-preservation advised him from revealing his hiding place. Pepito tried to see as much as he could but he did not see the faces of the two men because everything went fast, but in his mind he engraved one little thing that caught his attention, and that was a little mark on the back of the black boots worn by one of the men, which mark, he thought, was a small, flaming red cross.

Having made sure that the men had gone, Pepito went to his father and tried to bring him to, all the time crying and sobbing and talking to his father. This went on for some time until Pepito finally realized that his father was not going to talk to him, or move anymore, for he remembered that when an animal was killed at the hacienda, the animal did not move anymore, either. Little by little, Pepito's weeping and sobbing went away and a new emotion took hold of his entire being – fear of the unknown.

He was not hungry, there was plenty of food in his father's "mochila" (knapsack); and he was not thirsty, there was plenty of cool, clean water; the sun was shining brightly, so he could not be afraid of the dark; then, he wondered why he did not know what to do. His mind finally began to put his situation in perspective and then a number of thoughts assailed him in profusion. It would be dark in a few hours; he could not stay in that place for a long time; there was a chance he could be attacked by a wild cat or some other animal; he did not trust himself to know the way home; and he could not get on the horse. As much as his mind told him to stay by his father hoping that somebody would come, his instinct forced him to act; and to this effect he started looking for a low hanging branch to try to get on his father's horse, but when he managed to untie it, the horse started to walk at a slow pace. When Pepito saw the horse the horse moving he thought that maybe the horse knew the way home, for he remembered that sometimes when riding both he and his father would doze off and the horse kept going as if it knew the way home. Pepito grabbed hold of one of the reins and tried to keep pace with the horse whose slow pace was still faster than his walk. After about three hours of hard walking the horse and Pepito arrived home.

JOSÉ VALDEZ

Pepito was so spent from his ordeal and the long walk home that when he arrived at the stables he dropped to the ground and in an instant was dead to the world. Antonio, the stable boy, tried to wake him but could not, so he ran to the house and at the kitchen door met Juana and told her about Pepito. Juana thought it very strange that Pepito was sleeping on the hay at the stable and asked Antonio about Martin. Antonio could not offer any more information, so Juana went to Doña Virginia's bedroom to give her Luis and tell her about Pepito. Doña Virgina took the baby and Juana ran to the stables to find out what had happened to Martin and Pepito Juana picked up Pepito who half-awakened embraced his mother and started crying. When Juana asked about his father, Pepito answered that there were two men, and there was a fight, and the men left and his father did not move and there was lost so blood on the ground. Juana asked where the place was but Pepito only knew that his father said something about going towards El Cesteadero.

Juana heard enough and went to find Don Carlos. Don Carlos knew where the place was and after putting on his coat of mail and sword in case of trouble, jumped on his horse and started at a gallop accompanied by two of his men. When he arrived at El Cesteadero horror filled his face at the sight of Martin lying in a pool of blood, his face contorted and his lips half open in his last desperate effort to talk to his son, and his eyes open with a blank stare. Don Carlos closed Martin's eyes and walked around where the fight had taken place trying to find some tell-tale sign of foot prints or marks left by the hooves of the horses of the assassins but found nothing.

20

Don Carlos Suspects the Twins
– And Doña Manuela Gives
Birth to Felipe, Jr

After wrapping the body of his trusted employee and friend in blankets which he had taken for that purpose, Don Carlos started the long ride home, all the while wondering who could have perpetrated such a dastardly crime for as far as he knew, Martin was an easy going person, kind and considerate, who had no enemies. Don Carlos was experiencing a very high amount of frustration and anger, and he would use all means at his disposal to try to find out who the killers were and bring them to justice no matter who they were or what it cost.

When Don Carlos returned to the hacienda he found Juana trying to calm Pepito. Don Carlos, them, tried to get busy doing various things which had to be done in connection with

Martin's death, and all that, prevented him from undertaking the most sad and difficult task of telling Juana and also his own wife the terrible fate that had befallen Martin. He had to send for Doctor Bragelone to make official the cause of death; he sent for a priest to give Martin's remains a Christian buriel; also, he had to notify the alcalde so that Martin's name be made part of statistics; and finally, the number of original Indians in his encomienda had to be reduced by one. There was also, the terrible task of finding the best way to break the horrifying news to Juana and Doña Virginia both of whom were already feeling dread and apprehension from wondering about the absence of Martin.

After taking care of all those unfortunate but necessary duties, including notifying Juana and his wife about Martin's death which caused the two women to cry inconsolably, Don Carlos sent for Pepito to try to obtain more information which would point to assassins. When Don Carlos asked Pepito where he had been when the struggle happened, Pepito answered that his father had told him to hide in the tall reeds by the edge of the water, and not to come out no matter what happened. Pepito was asked again to describe the two men, and he told Don Carlos that they seemed to be a little taller than his father, had long capes that almost covered their faces, and carried long swords like Don Carlos. Pepito was further asked if the two men called each other by name and he answered in the negative, and could not offer any more information.

The police were notified and they started looking all over La Morada for anybody with a machete wound on the left arm but without success. Something kept bothering Don

Carlos and to that effect he began inquiring very discreetly about Doña Manuela's brothers but was told that on the day before the terrible incident, the Twins had left La Morada and were in the town of Toluca trying to close a business transaction. Teodoro and Doroteo had wind of Don Carlos' investigation, so they decided to prolong their stay in Toluca until Doroteo's wound had healed completely.

Don Felipe and Doña Manuela visited Don Carlos and Doña Virginia and offered their condolences; and Doña Manuela also commiserated with Juana and even offered any kind of help that she would need. Juana courteously thanked her but for the moment, she told her, she did not need anything for Don Carlos and Doña Virginia had been kind enough to tend to her every need. Doña Manuela seemed a little mollified because she thought she felt a certain aloofness on Juana's part, her desire being to gain a little rapport with Juana in order to get closer to get closer to baby Luis. Doña Manuela did not give up, however, and promised herself to find a way to gain Juana's confidence. For the present, however, she would have to hold her plans in abeyance because she was not in a position to do much traveling not even to visit neighbors, for her time was approaching.

As it happened, on the day after her visit to Doña Virginia she gave birth to a baby boy, the date being October 6, 1530, who was named Felipe, after his father, and as an endearing term was to be called Pito. This time it was Don Carlos and Doña Virginia who went to Don Felipe's estancia, as he wanted his place to be referred to, and offered their congratulations on the new addition to their family, while

JOSÉ VALDEZ

inwardly they knew they had for the moment done the right thing for their own offspring. They also knew that they were going to lead a life, not only difficult but also subject to sanctions on account of the masquerade that could create confusion in the records of New Spain and the annals of the Spanish Empire.

21

A Doting Mother For a Snobbish Son

In the fall of 1542 Teodoro and Doroteo, who had continued their life of leisure, drinking and dissolution, had gained control of the wayward element in La Morada to the point that anybody who somehow had escaped unwanted visitors, lived in fear of becoming the next victims. Very few people went out of their homes because everybody began to notice that it was almost uncanny that the crooks always knew the exact time to strike. There were also too many attacks in broad daylight and that had to be stopped or else everybody was going to take matters into his own hands and anarchy would follow. When it seemed that somebody had to act, Don Carlos spearheaded a demand that Mexico City send investigators to find the head or heads of the criminal element, and to stop all the atrocities being committed by persons that nobody knew because their deeds were conducted at night.

The influence that Don Carlos still enjoyed finally decided the ministers in charge in the capital to do something about the situation for they feared Don Carlos would be sure to go directly to the Viceroy, so they sent a squad of ten soldiers under the command of Captain Julio Montes, and a justice of the peace by the name of Noten Robando. This continent was furnished headquarters by Don Carlos in a small but adequate building which he had set aside for this particular purpose; this facility being situated in the middle of the only avenue the few businesses had been established.

No sooner had this police delegation set up their property business or personal, than the Twins came to welcome them and to assure them of their desire to contribute in any way to make their stay comfortable and to help in their investigations. Obviously the new arrivals accepted the Twins' offer especially when dined with the best viands and liquor in La Morada by two of the best-known citizens.

To say that the Twins had gained the confidence of the police group is to minimize a fact, because by continuing to shower Captain Montes and his men with gifts, including money which the soldiers showed no compunction in accepting, Teodoro and Doroteo, to all intents and purposes became part of the law-enforcing and investigating factions. This of course revealed to the Twins the plans and activities of the police, which to begin with, became lax in their assigned duties, and that made it easy for Teodoro and Doroteo to continue their chosen line of nocturnal activities at the most opportune times.

Even though they seemed to be and go everywhere, the Twins managed somehow to avoid visiting Don Carlos Hacienda, and for a good reason. In their minds was the fear that Pepito might remember them, because there was always talk about Pepito being hidden in the reeds when they had killed Martin, and they were not about to take a chance in a confrontation. When the police group came from the capital, everybody including Don Carlos, expected the situation to take a turn for the better but there did not seem to make too much difference. When things did not show improvement, Don Carlos and other citizens noticed that Teodoro and Doroteo were becoming entirely too friendly with the police, and Don Carlos' suspicions were additionally fueled by noticing that Teodoro and Doroteo never ran into any trouble with the criminal element even though they kept most unusual hours day or night, and their abode was never visited by any light fingered gentry, but for the moment the only thing he could do was keep a close eye on the pair.

Up to the Fall 1542, a period of about 12 years, the lives of all persons that merit interest in this narrative proceeded in accordance with their abilities, talents and the ever present factor of luck, good or bad. Life, if not ideal, at best became tolerable. The family of Don Carlos prospered, and the family of Don Felipe suffered a few setbacks but those did not bother Doña Manuela because her entire life, her heaven on hearth was wrapped around her son Felipe, Jr. Felipe, Jr. was a stocky boy following his mother's characteristics rather than his father's, and his men tended to be on the haughty side. He never let an opportunity pass to tell his classmates and all that would listen, rather pointedly at Luis if he was present, that although his father was quite famous because of his military exploits, his mother was a direct descendant from one of the most Castizo (noble descent) families of Madrid. Obviously, his behavior did not earn him many friends but that did not bother him at all; and being of a quick temper he was left alone, which suited him well.

Although related, Pito and Luis kept their relationship at a minimum, it bothered Pito that sometimes he felt as if Luis just as soon ignore him. Pito tried to draw Luis into any kind of conversation but without much success for Luis answered only when the conversation covered general subjects, and would skillfully avoid personal questions or reference to family matters, pleading ignorance, which course of action always facilitated terminating the conversation. After awhile Pito and Luis fell into a mutual practice of accepting each other and at the same time politely ignoring each other.

22

Doña Manuela Continues Day Dreaming and Planning - Luis and Pito 12 Years Old

Don Felipe had lapsed more and more into a life of intoxication and lassitude which was not doing his system much good; and the vice of smoking which he had picked up in the last three years compounded the sad state of his health, by a pernicious cough which shook him quite violently at times. Don Carlos, in an effort to offer his cousin some distraction, would invite him to a game of boliche, a ride in the hills or a dip in the cool water of one of the many small lakes in the area, but not with much success.

Since her husband was not much for conversation anymore, preferring solitude and pulque to her company and that of Felipe, Jr., Doña Manuela, whether she had planned it that

JOSÉ VALDEZ

way or not, was left in complete charge of the Estancia, as Don Felipe liked to call his holdings. To make matters somewhat more difficult, even her intimate life was practically gone for Don Felipe suffered a sever case of mumps around late 1540, which rendered him sterile; and this last setback contributed to his moodiness and depression, and did not follow Doctor Bragelone's advice to fortify his system by good, clean food and to stay away from pulque and tobacco.

This turn in her life forced Doña Manuela to look for other outlets for her unbounded energy, two of which were keeping up with the society of the capital and being a doting mother to Felipe, Jr., by granting him his every wish and desire; and this attitude spoiled Pito all the more. In her few moments of solace and reverie disturbing thoughts would assail her, spoiling her moment of peace and rest. She would visualize her Pito and Luis and would compare one against the other; but there was doubt – her Pito was born to rule over the domain she had always envisioned and to which she had dedicated most of her life.

Doña Manuela would attribute to Pito a strong character and a ruthless disposition, which qualities were indispensable for success. Luis? – well, Doña Manuela saw him with his soft manners, natty apparel and well developed but somewhat delicate frame, as a dandy who would eventually perish in the strife of life. However, while day dreaming she would sometimes be jolted into reality by the unacceptable thought that all she had strived for, fought for and was ever planning for, would be a blow she could not stand, if somehow Luis outlived her son. When thoughts like these overwhelmed her, a faint but nefarious solution would stay in her mind for a fleeting moment.

As far as Pepito was concerned, his life had fallen into a humdrum existence, and his lot was just a little better than the life of the other members of the encomienda because his mother was still working in the kitchen, and at times taking care of Luis who by now was twelve years old. One thing that was beyond Pepito's comprehension was why his mother still had to, most of the time, taken care of Luis, when in his opinion, at twelve years of age and well developed, Luis should have been able to take care of himself. Something else he did not understand was that he used to have the run of the hacienda, and when he started growing and developing, Don Carlos gave orders for him to come to visit his mother only at certain times; and for that purpose Juana and Pepito were assigned accommodation in a small but adequate cabin that had been used for storing agricultural tools. The place was well ventilated and supplied with the minimum but necessary furniture and other articles.

Juana still spent most of the day in Don Carlos' mansion and only returned when allowed time to rest, and at those times she would prepare and take care of Pepito's clothes, and also prepare meals for him. Juana's and Pepito's quarters were located just outside a compound which included the sprawling house, buildings used for various purposes, storage sheds and the stables which housed the horses and mules stalls; all of the foregoing being protected by a thick adobe wall about nine feet high which was in crusted with broken glass and other sharp objects designed to impede into Don Carlos' property by other than the customary entrance.

JOSÉ VALDEZ

23

Pepito Has Questions But No Answers - Luis Wants To Be A Swordsman

From the time Pepito's close contact with his mother was curtailed which was about the time of the birth of Luis, and he was about 4 years old, he sensed that there was something he could not understand. He noticed that somehow Don Carlos and Doña Virginia, and even his own mother did not want him around when Juana was taking care of Luis. He could not find an answer so he thought that he had done something wrong and was being punished. He had seen babies before, of all types, the only difference was that Luis had a fair skin, so he did the only thing he knew to do – forget about things he did not understand, accept the new way of doing things and rearrange his habits as best as he could, and try to think about his father's death which at times seemed to bother him very much.

One day while trying to recollect as much as he could about the incident, one little piece of information that he had not thought about in some time made him realize that all the time he had been hiding in the reeds he had been looking for a face, but because of the fast and violent action he had not been able to form a picture in his mind; but there was something that had caught his attention, and that was what he thought was a small flaming red cross etched on the outside of the upper heel of jet black boots worn by the man who had killed his father. Since that was the only concrete item that he could remember, it became an obsession for Pepito to search for markings on Spaniards only on their footwear for he knew that mestizos and Indians could only afford huaraches.

Considering that Luis was not a boy, she was of average height for a boy, but, of course, quite tall for a girl for she had inherited her mother's physical endowments. Don Carlos and wife knew that they had imposed upon themselves a quite difficult task bringing Luis up as a boy, but received a most pleasant surprise when almost from the beginning Luis began to show qualities displayed by a boy rather than a girl. Don Carlos and Doña Virginia by dint of repetition and careful explaining prevailed upon her (Luis) that she dress like a boy because otherwise she would not be allowed to pursue boys' endeavors, and such activities such as practice of arms, which was something she wanted to do ever since she could remember.

JOSÉ VALDEZ

Eventually, Luisa acquired a boy's identity and as Doña Virginia pointed out to her she would be inherently protected from pranks and tricks played on girls by unruly boys. By the time Luis was eight, he had already begun to ride horses, knew how to arm and disarm an harquebus and would go out on the fields close by to hunt small game with a honda which an Indian boy had given him, and which Luis learned to use with great accuracy. All in all, Luis was rounding out into a very active and athletic boy that made his father very proud.

As Don Carlos had kept up with his swordsmanship by daily practice with a master swordsman friend of his, Luis would watch fascinated by the unbelievable lightning fast strokes of the adversaries, and the clashing of the swords sounded like music to Luis, and he thought it all so beautiful and exciting that he would daydream about the time when he would be good enough to measure his weapon against that of anybody. In order to learn more about the art of fencing Luis would spend hours reading some books that his father treasured and would memorize the different strokes and maneuvers described. After a time Don Carlos let him handle a light foil in order to teach him the fundamentals of the art. Luis, although of rather light build, was wiry and with quite strong hands, wrists, arms and legs due to constant exercise which developed his physique; and after a few practices Don Carlos was amazed at the natural dexterity of his son. By the time Luis reached the age of twelve, although not a consummate swordsman, Luis felt that he could take care of himself in an emergency, and his father and mother agreed and were happy with his exploits.

24

*Unwittingly, Pepito
Discovers Luis' Secret*

It was around this time that a very significant incident took place that was to affect many people, but of everyone involved, none was more affected than Luis and Pepito (the latter to be called later in life either Pepe or José, his true name). This incident happened in the month of July of a season that was to be talked about as one of the hottest in many years. Don Carlos had diverted the running water from one of several canals emanating from the hills nearby, for the purpose of building a small pool. The flow of water was to be controlled by a floodgate at the bottom of the adobe wall so that the water of the pool could be renewed at necessary intervals. This pool served to give members of his family a respite from

JOSÉ VALDEZ

the very warm weather by taking a dip in the cool waters of the pool.

On almost every afternoon Doña Virginia and Luis would go to the pool to refresh themselves, but on this occasion since everybody was busy in their endeavors, Luis decided to take a dip in the pool by himself, unaware that she was being watched by somebody on the outside of the adobe wall.

On the next day of school, as he was returning home, Luis was accosted by Pepito who asked him to listen to what he had to say. Luis told Pepito to go ahead and speak, but Pepito, in a low voice and in a somewhat embarrassing countenance told Luis the following; "Luis, I am very sorry and ashamed about what I have to tell you. It was never my intention to snoop on anybody, and after I make this confession to you, I know I will be in deep trouble. I do not know how to make amends, but one thing I want you to be sure, and that is that I do not want to know the reason why you impersonate a boy, and also, that if my life depends on keeping your secret, I will gladly forfeit it".

"Pepito, what is it you are trying to tell me? I seem to have a rough idea, but the most important and at the same time quite interestingly is how and when you discovered that I am not a boy. Please continue for I am anxious to listen to your explanation", she told him.

After a short pause during which Pepito seemed to be looking for words that would make his confession more acceptable, he began – "After my day's work yesterday, as I was walking along the wall, I noticed a place on the wall that seemed to be quite deteriorated, or that perhaps someone had been trying to pierce or perforate. On closer inspection I discovered that there was a slit no bigger than the head of a pin. The natural thing was to find out if one could see anything on the inside, and when I tried to look, to my amazement and also discomfort, I happened to see you, and that is how I started to wonder why you always wear boy's apparel."

"Pepito", she answered, "I am somewhat dismayed and frustrated because of my parents' instructions to come to the pool accompanied either by my mother or Juana, and as far as the reason why I always wear boy's clothing, I do not know why, except that they must have very strong reasons, and besides, I like things the way they are. You know, of course, that I am going to have to tell my parents about all this."

"If you wish to continue being a boy, not only is it your privilege but to me, if that is your wish, you will always be Luis. However, as far as telling your family about all this, I hope they understand that it was never my intention to be in a situation that I consider precarious and also disturbing because my future, as insignificant as I expect it to be, rests entirely in the hands of your father and your mother. However, if you choose not to tell them, I swear to you that I will keep your secret even if my life should depend on my silence", he replied.

"Pepito, If I may use this expression, the damage has been done, and in a way, it is good that it was you and not somebody else that my family and I could not be relied upon to keep my secret. For the moment, to prevent a repetition of another similar incident, two things come to my mind that have to be done – repair the wall now, and tell my parents

JOSÉ VALDEZ

because I have never kept anything from them. My father is just and will know what to do," she told him.

"I understand, Luis, and the only favor I ask is that I be present when you tell them".

"If you like, let us go now", she told him.

25

Don Carlos Gives His Decision
And Pepito changes Residence

Together they entered by the front entrance and Pepito waited in the anteroom, where his mother who had opened the door for them, approached him to find out what was happening but Pepito would not answer except to tell his mother to pray for him because he was in trouble. A short time later Luis called him from the living room, where Don Carlos and Doña Virginia were already waiting; and after Pepito entered, Luis closed the door, leaving Juana in a very apprehensive mood. An embarrassing pause ensued until Don Carlos broke his silence, "Luis or Pepito, if you have anything to tell us, we are waiting."

Luis tried to talk, "Mother, I don't know how to begin.

"It cannot be that bad, Luis, for I can see that there is nothing unusual between you two. Maybe Pepito should tell us," her mother told her.

"Doña Virginia, with all due respect, I think that Luis should explain the situation", Pepito replied.

Doña Virginia continued, "Well, Luis, what happened that seems to trouble you so much, to say nothing of Pepito who also seems to be out of sorts".

Don Carlos was becoming impatient, "Luis, it cannot have anything to do with school because Pepito does not attend your school."

"Father, what I am going to say is very embarrassing to us and I hope that you will take into consideration the most unusual set of circumstances involving this incident," Luis began.

"Anybody would think this is a matter of life and death. Please begin, Luis," he asked.

"I don't know if this is a matter of life and death, father, but Pepito has discovered our secret", Luis blurted out.

"As your mother, Luis, I assure you I have no idea what secret you are talking about."

"Mother, I regret to tell you and father that the secret we are talking about is the one that makes me Luis instead of Luisa."

"Not that, Luis!"

"Yes, father, that one."

At this point Doña Virginia became visibly excited and she turned to Luis and Pepito several times before she started to ask them, "How did it happen, Luis? How did you ever find out, Pepito? Will somebody please explain?"

Turning to his wife Don Carlos told her, "This is a very serious matter, and because it is so important, we have to know every detail in order to guide our lives accordingly."

It was his turn, so Luis said, "To start with, yesterday I went to the pool by myself because it was very warm, and neither mama nor Juana were available."

Don Carlos interrupted, "Where were you, Virginia?"

Doña Virginia answered, "I went to the kitchen for a few minutes, Carlos, to talk to Juana about supper, and I may have taken fifteen or twenty minutes, but I expected Luis to be waiting for me to help her with the change of clothing."

"I'm sorry, Mama," Luis apologized. Don Carlos then turned to Pepito, "You haven't told us your side of the story, Pepito."

"Don Carlos," Pepito explained, "As I told Luis when he was returning from school, I was walking along the wall headed this way because I wanted to talk to my mother, when I happened to notice a place on the wall where it seemed as if somebody had started to dig a hole, and natural curiosity drove me to look through a slit no bigger than the eye of a needle."

Don Carlos stated, "I will not ask for any more details, but if you looked and saw, what is to keep somebody else from doing the same?"

"Not feasible, Carlos," advised Doña Virginia, "because if that had happened, the word would be out, especially as it concerns Doña Manuela. Also, this took place a little after one hour after lunch, more or less, when the children are in school and the older folks are taking a siesta."

"Pepito, how come you were around?" Doña Virginia added. Pepito answered the question with noticeable embarrassment

JOSÉ VALDEZ

that was apparent by the color on his face," I was coming to see my mother about a remedy because of a stomach problem." "I hope your mother took care of your problem, but in the meantime two things must be taken care of immediately," added Don Carlos, "the first one is to repair the wall now, and the second is to make sure that Pepito does not have occasion to talk at length with the other boys from the encomienda, and the only way, in my opinion, is to keep Pepito out of school and under the watchful eye of Juana."

"But Don Carlos, I swear on my father's grave." Pepito told him.

Don Carlos responded, "No, Pepito, you are twelve years old and by now you are almost through all the schooling you are allowed to attend. Besides, I see no other recourse, so my decision stands. You can help around this place in a lot of ways, helping your mother in the kitchen, or wherever there is need of help; bringing wood; looking after the horses we keep inside for emergency, and making sure they are well taken care of, etc. I am going to notify the overseers that you are not to work outside anymore."

26

True Friendship Develops Between Luis and Pepe - Pepe Breaks Down A Barrier

As time went on, Luis, at twelve years of age could be proud of two accomplishments, one of which was his dexterity with a sword, something that she thought could not be matched by anyone under the age of sixteen, and that included Pepe, who by pestering Luis to teach him how to handle a sword, had, himself made great strides with a sword which Luis borrowed from his father's collection. The other accomplishment was teaching Pepe to read and write acceptably, which only proved that either Luis was a good teacher, or Pepe a very intelligent pupil, or both.

Don Carlos had no idea what Luis and Pepe had been doing the last few years, and to his great surprise, when he stayed home one morning instead of taking a long stroll which would take him close to lunch time, or traveling to Mexico City to keep up with the news and old friends, or conversing with a few cronies at his favorite tavern, he heard that familiar clash of steel. He went to the door leading to the patio, next to the dining room, and he saw Luis and Pepe fencing on even terms, with each trying to take advantage of the other's weakness, even taunting each other, and in general both them having a very good time. Although the point of the swords were protected by a button; each mark or "toque" was bound to leave a small welt in the place of contact in the body, neither Luis or Pepe paid any attention and continued their practice until they saw that Don Carlos was watching them quite intently.

Luis spoke first, "Father, I needed someone to help me with my practice and Pepe does pretty good."

Don Carlos then spoke to Pepe, "I can see that, but being a good swordsman will not do you much good because you will never be allowed to measure yourself against an opponent or enter a "justa" (joust) because of your station in life. However, I do not deny you the privilege of fencing with Luis because this and other things that I do for you now and will do in the future, I do in memory of Martin, your father, who was the best worker and one of the best friends I have ever had. While both of you are pretty good, with Luis the situation is different for he can take lessons from the Master of Arms and taste excellence; but if I ask the Master of Arms to do the same for you, he will refuse because if he agrees he will be the laughing stock of the community."

After Don Carlos finished giving Pepe what he thought was good advice, Pepe spoke in a tone that left no doubt in Don Carlos' mind how he felt about being a member of a lower level of society, "I am very thankful for everything you have done for me, Don Carlos, and I would like to find a way to repay you, something that will be very difficult to do because, as you say, we belong to different levels of society. I have a feeling, however, that sometime, somehow, I will have a chance to prove I can be anybody's equal."

"I know you can do it, Pepe," Luis agreed with a certain amount of enthusiasm, "and as far as the matter of the Master of Arms, I will try to teach you whatever I learn from him."

"Pepe," Don Carlos said, "I have no more to say except that I have no objection, so far, to the relationship you two have created, but if at any time you trespass the boundaries of propriety, you will leave me no choice but to have you exiled so that you are never seen around these parts again."

"Thank you, father," Luis told him.

"Thank you, Don Carlos," Pepe said.

Since to all intents and purposes the barrier that had naturally existed which had prevented Pepe from establishing any sort of closeness or intimacy with Luis had been broken by Don Carlos, whenever Pepe found some difficulty with his upper classman studies, (he was not permitted to attend such classes), he would look for Luis for help, during a break in his work.

On the other hand, Luis would take advantage of a school break to watch Pepe work, and at times, would even try to help him so that Pepe would get his chores done so that they could practice their swordsmanship. All in all, given their natural needs, Luis and Pepe enjoyed their convenient relationship which was to develop ever so slowly into a true and close friendship.

JOSÉ VALDEZ

27

Pepe Does Not Understand Nature, And Luis Becomes Ambidextrous

When Luis passed his twelfth year and was a few days from his thirteenth, some people within the household began to see him in a different light, his mother and Juana. Pepe, also when almost seventeen, began to have thoughts of a most disturbing nature, which to that point had been unperceived by him, when he started noticing that Luis was undergoing a change that he could not explain to himself

Doña Virginia ever since Luis had passed her twelfth year had been watching him for tell-tale signs of upper body development; and now that he was almost thirteen and the signs had made their appearance she redoubled her observations having already explained to Luis all that he had to know about the monthly ritual, injecting a bit of her humor by advising Luis that being on guard did not necessarily refer only to the art of swordsmanship. On his part Luis, being right handed began to notice an ever so slight shortening of his "a fondo" (lunge) thrust when he practiced such maneuver against a man-size dummy.

Luis went to his mother and both of them apprised Don Carlos of the new developments, and he offered some simple but practical solutions. Luis should wear, he advised, a doublet of very light material that will not hamper natural movement, but of metallic character that can stand any blow of average force. A contraption to satisfy those requirements was fashioned by an artisan friend of Don Carlos. Another advantage, if it can be so considered, was to inhibit in some measure the development of that part of the body that it served to protect. The other simple solution that was given by Don Carlos concerning the technical part of the slight shortening of thrust or lunge noticed by Luis, was to get closer to the subject. This correction could offer more accuracy, but at the same time, on the drawback side, allows the same advantage to the adversary, making this type of adjustment a matter of discretion or timing during the match.

It did not take Luis long to adjust to the new equipment, nor for Pepe to catch up with the lessons learned from the Master of Arms by Luis, who more and more developed such agility and dexterity that he soon gained the reputation of being one of the best, if not the best, pupils at the academy. Although Luis, himself, felt quite comfortable sparring with any of the other pupils, there was one in particular that always seemed to give him quite a bit of trouble. Pablo, the boy's name, had absolute confidence in his ability, and did not mind telling all the other students how good he was, and at every opportunity would belittle anybody's efforts. .

In time, whether he wanted it or not, Luis acquired a faction that considered him their champion; while the other half of the students considered Pablo "El Zurdo" (lefty) their champion. On his side Pablo had Felipe, Jr. who, because of his largesse with the money made available to him by his mother, helped a solid front for his friend, Pablo, "El Zurdo." As much as Luis tried to stay away or remain aloof of what he considered childish behavior, at times he felt as if he could not stand the sardonic laugh, the barbs and asides which Pito and Pablo hurled at each other with a double meaning, and intended for Luis and his friends. As this situation seemed to continue to the point when it was becoming unbearable, Luis finally saw that the only way to silence Pablo was by completely dominating his style of play, something that he was not sure he could just yet because of Pablo's unorthodox style of play.

Wrestling with this problem, Luis went to his father, who as usual, had some ready advice for him. Don Carlos told Luis that under similar circumstance, and if he could go back in time, he would fight fire with fire. In the first place, he added, if it bothers you that your opponent is left handed, think about the fact that by the same token you being right handed should bother him, also. On the other hand, if you think you have sufficient ability and confidence, learn left handed swordsmanship, which should not take long if you practice for hours in front of a full-length mirror. Luis followed his father's advice and very little time he felt he was making very good progress in his new endeavor, and not surprisingly, Pepe was also advancing at the same pace.

28

Luis Wrestles With Convention

Pepe, at seventeen, had developed into a muscular young man, taller than the average, fairly good looking, with a grave look on his face that made him look older than his true age; and with a walk, never a swagger, that exuded assurance and confidence which he acquired, possibly, from the inner knowledge that he was making strides into the world of the Spaniards. Pepe's friendship and companionship with Luis was still there but seemed to be drifting into a reserved attitude because he was realizing that Luis had undergone a change that somehow demanded of him a different conduct; and he also reasoned that the time was approaching when both would no longer be able to talk to each other on a first name basis.

JOSÉ VALDEZ

As far as Luis was concerned, he felt some difference in Pepe's attitude, not because she was thinking of convention, but because she was seeing a Pepe that she had not seen before. Pepe, was he, who not too long ago had gone into the woods and the open fields with him, and showed him the kinds of edible fruits which the majority of Spaniards were still very cautious about tasting, let alone eating —like the zapote, chaote, tejocote and mamey. Pepe had shown him to use the honda (slingshot) and marveled at the accuracy displayed. Luis remembered many other things he had learned from Pepe, and how it seemed to her that Pepe was always there when she needed him.

Now, however, there he was, a full-grown man, of very good build, of easy and fluid movements, and a good sparring partner. She was beginning to realize that even on the strength or merit of all these things, Pepe seemed to be slipping away, and she had no idea how to stop this tendency. She did not want to approach the subject or press Pepe for an explanation of what she thought was a slight reserve in their relationship, but she felt that it was not up to her, and anyway, she hoped things would somehow go to what they were before; but something was prodding her in her mind to try to understand that the society of which she was a privileged member had a neat place for everybody; a place where nobody was allowed to stray from unless a price commensurate to the change desired, was paid. Luis would rebel at the rules of such convention which showed that he was beginning to have a mind of his own, and even though she realized the nature of the obstacles facing her, she made up her mind that she would not submit to the convention that was threatening to take away from her the best friend she ever had, and that would not happen if she had any say in the matter.

Possibly what was making Luis take a definite stance in the matter of her friendship with Pepe was another aspect of the situation that assailed him at times was a thought that he had relegated to the back of her mind, or refused to dwell upon, a thought that she considered very strange because it appeared only when she was close to Pepe. Although she had grown well beyond her grown well beyond her age, without knowing it she was still trying to cling to the boyhood that had been, up to then, the happiest period in her life; and that was perhaps, the reason why her heart beat a little faster and a sort of well being enveloped her when Pepe was close to her, or spoke to her; but she was not sure that was the correct explanation.

Luis and Pepe, to all intents and purposes, had at fourteen and eighteen years respectively attained their full physical development and had shed practically all vestiges of childhood. Pepe had been placed in an overseer capacity of personnel who performed various jobs within the compound. As he gained influence, he also gained the admiration and respect of his own people and even, however grudgingly, of some friends of Don Carlos, who had heard of Pepe's talents and exploits, and also approved of the way Pepe comported himself and "kept his place." Not withstanding all his attributes.

There were many others who disliked him because of jealousy and plain envy because of his Indian heritage, and at the top of the list were Teodoro and Doroteo who were instrumental in having Pepe run off the neighborhood tavern where Pepe had gone, as was his custom to look for any

Spaniard wearing black boots with a small flaming red cross on the back of the heel. Pepe did not forget such shabby treatment and promised himself to repay the Twins at the earliest opportunity. In the meantime he went to find Luis to tell him that he thought he had found the man with the black boots with a flaming red cross on the back of the heel. When asked by Luis who the man in question was, Pepe answered that it was Teodoro.

29

Is it a Cross, An "F", Or A "T?"
– Their Conscience Bothers the Twins

Although young in years, Luis displayed unusual insight when he made Pepe realize that great care and tact had to be exercised in this situation because the Twins were brothers of Doña Manuela, wife of Don Felipe and that in a manner of speaking made her Don Carlos' sister-in-law, and the Twins, sadly enough, and by he same extension, related to Don Carlos, also. Luis added that there could be others with the same characteristics, and besides, how could you, or I, or anybody else know for sure that the marking in question was a red cross when it could be a monogram like, for example a "T or even an "F".

When Luis mentioned a "T", Pepe remembered that the boots and the flaming red cross that he had always had in

JOSÉ VALDEZ

his mind were worn by Teodoro whose given name starts with a "T". As Pepe and Luis kept thinking about the possibility that Teodoro could be the person Pepe had been searching for, the question came up as to how to ascertain if in fact it was a "T" on the boots that Teodoro wore, for that would make him a prime suspect in the murder of Martin, Pepito's father. Further deliberation resulted in a decision to ask Don Carlos for advice about what seemed to be at least circumstantial evidence, and the problem of getting close enough to Teodoro to make sure the supposed cross was in reality a "T".

If Pepe and Luis expected a definite sign of support from Don Carlos, they were sorely disappointed because Don Carlos made them see the situation exactly the way it was up to that poing. In the first place, he said, even if it were true, which I myself doubt, it would be Pepe's word against Teodoro's; and as it concerns Teodoro and his twin, despite their reprehensible conduct at times, it is very difficult to think that either of them would be capable of committing such a vile deed. Again, he proceeded, even if the case came to trial, the very fact that an Indian accuses a Spanish Caballero is enough to throw the case out of court. Finally, it has been around fourteen years since the crime was committed, and a lot of people would doubt that a four year old boy could remember the incident after such a long period of time. I regret that I do not have anything better to offer, but that is the way things are; however, and for what it is worth, if you come up with more information, please let me know, and by the same token, if I come across anything at all, I will advise both of you immediately.

Ever since the news broke out that at the time of the crime Pepito had been hiding in th ereeds and rushes, and was therefore not only a witness but someone who could identify the assassins, Teodoro and Doroteo began to have misgivings about whether Pepe could identify them. After some time, when things returned to normal and the hiding of Pepito had been forgotten, Teodoro tried to convince his brother that there was no way that Pepe could remember them if he actually saw the, which he doubted, because their capes, even during the fray, covered their faces which they had tried to hide from their victim, Martin.

Doroteo, however, had doubts because he was sure that when he fell from his wounded horse his face was uncovered and he could have been recognized; which was not the case because the boy's sight at that precise moment was centered on Teodoro who was about to kill Pepe's father with a thrust of his sword. As time went on, and Pepe was assigned work on the fiels and sometimes within the compound, every time the Twins happened to see him the suspicions that had lain dormant for a long time would once more come to the surface and become quite bothersome, but Pepe went about his job seemingly paying no undue attention to them.

After Luis and Pep had discussed the matter of Teodoro's boots and the red cross or red ltter, which situation had to lay in abeyance until its resolution, Pepe, in his mind became sure that the Twins wee responsible for his father's death, and would dream about an opportunity to take matters in his hand, an action which would have been foolhardy and without any strong basis. At the same time Teodoro and Doroteo did not have a strong enough reason to effect a confrontation because

JOSÉ VALDEZ

in the first place nobody had accused them of anything, and secondly, Pepe was in the protection and vigilance of Don Carlos, so all things were to remain unsolved until something would precipitate action on either side.

30

*Doroteo Continues to Worry
– Pito and Luis Reach Semifinals
in Fencing Tournament*

Things remaining on the quiet side, a feeling of disquiet began to pervade the atmosphere of the households of Don Carlos and Don Felipe as if some unexpected trouble was about to disturb their usual uneventful life. The uneasy feeling which enveloped almost everybody, the reason for which nobody knew, was finally blamed on rumors without origin or solid foundation, that the names of the perpetrators of a crime committed fourteen years previously were going to be revealed. This, of course, made Doroteo quite jittery and it took all of his brother's persuasive arguments to calm his nerves. Teodoro would repeat ot his brother what to both of them would be their clinching point, and that was

JOSÉ VALDEZ

that no matter what developed, it would come to their word against that of an Indian whose recollection of the event in question which took place around fourteen years ago would be seriously questioned by everyone. Doroteo finally calmed his nerves having been convinced, one more time by his brother's reasoning.

To further allay his brother's fears and to help make him forget the unpleasant subject, Teodoro suggested attending the Master of Arms swordsmanship final matches. Doroteo agreed because Teodoro told him that Pito had reached the semifinals, and both of them were interested in how their nephew Felipe, Jr. performed. When they arrived, the preliminaries and the quarter final had already been completed, and only the group of semifinalists remained, which group comprised of Luis, Pablo the left handed whiz, Miguel, the son of a rich entrepreneur and Felipe Jr. The luck of the draw seemed to favor Pito (Felipe, Jr.) because his match was Miguel who was not expected to give Pito much trouble; and the other semifinal match, that almost everyone thought would eventually produce the winner of the tournament, pitted Pablo against Luis.

The spectators included the most influential members of the community, and of course, in the front row were Don Carlos and his wife Virginia, and Don Felipe and his wife Manuela, these last four being vitally interested in the last matches in which their offspring were participants. There were also, two important characters who for reasons of their own chose to be inconspicuous, the Twins, Teodoro and Doroteo.

The judges for the last matches having been chosen, the first semifinal was announced and the principals, Miguel and

Pito were called to the mat. After the rules were read and instructions given, Pito and Miguel took their places to await the signal from the Master of Arms. The match started in a whirlwind of action as if Pito meant to make short work of his adversary, scoring three quick points in the early minutes of the first ten-minute period. Although it was a fantastic start for anybody, Miguel was not about to let Pito run away with the match for he also aspired to a portion of the glory; so the first period ended with Pito ahead five points to four, both competitors short of the necessary seven points.

The second period started with an unexpected turn of events, as a desperate surge by Miguel gave him the lead in the match, a surprising six to five points advantage. According to the rules of the tournament, if no adversary attained the required seven points after two periods, more time would be allotted to the match until one of the participants emerged as the winner. This what Pito had in mind because the period was about to end. Miguel, who was so close to victory, in his anxiety and desperate lunges committed several glaring errors of which Pito took advantage by promptly scoring the sixth and the deciding point of the match, which gave rise to an audible sign of relief from Doña Manuela, Don Felipe and other relatives and friends or fans of Pito.

The second semifinal pitted the whiz kid, Pablo, against Luis, who was generally regarded as an elegant and possible the best pupil the Master of Arms had ever trained. At the beginning of the match, as the knowledgeable spectators had expected, each adversary started to feel the other to learn about the strategy as early as possible, while at the same time being very careful not to make an early mistake

JOSÉ VALDEZ

because between two equally gifted contestants being ahead by one point could be a definite advantage, and by two points, disastrous. The sympathy of the crowd seemed to be with the left handed Pablo who showed flashes of absolute confidence after having acquired a lead of two points to one in the first three minutes.

Luis, in the meantime remained calm and Don Carlos could tell that Luis was maneuvering Pablo into a position for a finesse move that Luis had practiced a number of times with Pepe. The result of the strategy was a quick point that wiped out the smile of confidence from Pablo's face. What had happened was that Pablo had tried some tricks of his own to counteract the new tactics of Luis, but as expected, the lack of confidence in executing something unfamiliar caused a lapse of concentration that eventually resulted in another quick point for Luis giving him the lead of three points to two. Luis, who knew that Pablo was not easily discouraged, doubled his energy to counteract Pablo's renewed efforts, but still the result showed, after furious attacks on both sides, in Luis losing another point which made the score at the end of the period three points to three.

31

Luis Reaches Finals After A Close Match

The match was renewed after the allowed rest period. Because Pablo was once more confident that his arm and wrist were stronger than those of Luis; he thought that the combination of heavier foil and stronger wrist and arm would eventually turn the tide in his favor, but he did not realize that by the same token the small difference in the weight of their weapons would work against his do-or-die effort because he was bound to get tired sooner. The match continued on even terms, but the best that Luis could muster under Pablo's relentless offensive was one point while Pablo could feel renewed confidence to the point of exhilaration when he scored two quick points with what he thought was relative ease.

Pablo began to feel victory within his grasp when Luis tripped while parrying a lunge from Pablo, and this caused Luis to lay prostrate and at the mercy of his adversary, and Pablo could have behaved in a chivalrous manner by allowing Luis to get up to continue the match, but instead took advantage of the situation, all within his right, and scored a mean "toque" in the middle of Luis' chest. All this merited an allowed rest during which the umpires and seconds discussed the situation and asked Luis if he wanted to yield, to which question he gave a resounding negative. The time spent in the second period was six and one half minutes leaving Pablo with what he reasoned was enough time to dispatch Luis, who seemed to have recovered sufficiently to continue.

It was at this point that a great hush enveloped the crowd when they saw that Luis, with exasperating calm, took the foil from his right hand and started doing warming exercises with his left arm. While Luis was doing his warming up exercises, Pablo's seconds protested the use of the left arm, but the ultimate decision was left to the Master of Arms who in rendering his verdict explained that the match was between two opponents and the pints were valid no matter what arm was used in the match. The signal for the continuation of the match was given but for one split second Pablo appeared so surprised that he did not obey the "en garde" command, and Luis had to wait until Pablo returned to reality.

After the match had resumed but before Pablo had fully recovered his composure, Luis had his way with his opponent's own technique, being left handed also, and by dividing his every move promptly tied the score at six points each, with only fifty seconds left in the match. At this juncture Pablo started to feel the effect of his own strategy for he began to tire, and Luis, feeling the difference when they clashed weapons, bided his time. At thirteen seconds left in the period Luis displayed such an array of short moves and lunges that left Pablo completely demoralized, befuddled and helpless to respond so that Luis in what could be called poetic retribution, landed a perfect "toque" in the middle of Pablo's chest for the seventh and deciding point thus ending his dreams of a championship as time ran out.

A thunderous applause greeted the victory of Luis who ran to his parents who were ecstatic, and were receiving from their friends and acquaintances congratulations for Luis' wonderful victory, and even Don Felipe and his wife congratulated them while at the same time experiencing misgivings about the pending final match of their son Pito with Luis who the concensus was that Luis was going to give Pito a lesson in the art of swordsmanship.

JOSÉ VALDEZ

32

Luis Defeats Pito For The Championship

When the principals in the match for the championship were called, Luis was asked if he desired more rest but he declined; and when Luis placed his weapon on the right hand, Don Felipe, Doña Manuela and the Twins and most of all, Pito, all sighed a sign of relief because that gave Pito a chance of making a better showing, also taking in consideration that the blow to Luis' upper arm left him at less than hundred percent competing ability.

The match began with everybody still wondering why Luis chose to fence right handed which had to be something of a handicap, instead of fencing left handed which could have given him an easy victory. What the spectators did not know was that for his hard and difficult match with Pablo, Luis did not warm up his muscles sufficiently and that put a strain on the muscles of his left forearm which caused cramps in the area of the tendons and muscles of the ulna and radius; and that naturally, had to affect the fluidity of movement.

This situation could have been disastrous if not for the fact that Pablo became completely disconcerted when Luis started beating him at his own game, so that Providence on his side, Luis practically just went through the motions to win his match with Pablo.

His match with Pito for the championship however, had a touch of psychology on both sides; Luis expected to win due to his previous mastery of Pito, and the latter saw a chance to give Luis a good match, never realizing how close he came to being the champion. Luis saw from the beginning that he could not afford to make any mistakes at all because any error could put him far back and catching up even to an adversary that was supposed to extend him, was unthinkable at the time.

The match dragged on with Luis neatly parrying all of Pito's sallies on all sides so that Pito was becoming exasperated and frustrated when he finally realized that Luis had not even tried any offense moves of his own. When he failed time and again to break through the defense that Luis made seem easy, he began to get careless and started to throw caution to the winds, which was exactly what Luis was waiting for by scoring two quick points.

Pito, instead of trying to regroup, as someone with a little more experience would have done, continued his foolish methods which, however, gained for him a point here and there, but which left Luis leading the match at five points to two. Despite his advantage Luis was not ready to claim victory

JOSÉ VALDEZ

so at this stage of the match Luis decided to go left handed which tactic completely demoralized Pito who practically gave up, allowing Luis to promptly score the last two points which gave him the victory and the championship. Recounting to his family the match with Pito, Luis confessed that scoring the clinching points happened not too soon because he was afraid that Pito would notice that he was wincing because of the pain, on every lunge or thrust to score.

Congratulations were in order for all contestants and the Master of Arms for having presented such an outstanding program, Don Carlos and Doña Virginia received congratulations from almost everybody except from the Twins who left as soon as the last match was over; and for their part, Don Carlos and Doña Virginia extended their congratulations to Don Felipe and Doña Manuela who could not hide her disappointment.

Don Carlos and his wife were fairly beaming with pride, and inwardly, when they looked at each other, their glances were meaningful and their message had to do with the fact that a young lady, their daughter, excelled in a sport dominated by males.

When Don Carlos, Doña Virginia and Luis returned home, Luis looked for Pepe to give him all the news about the fencing competition. Pepe listened intently to all details and was so happy that Luis had prevailed despite serious obstacles that he almost made a move as to embrace Luis, that she was hoping he would do, but Pepe checked his intention in time. These reactions, which were unnoticed by everybody except themselves, carried a tacit understanding that those type of emotions would not be restrained for too long.

33

Pepe Finally Finds The Boots With The "T" And Teodoro Has No Recource But To Accept Pepe's Challenge

While the fencing competition was going on, Pepe waited outside the building for he was not allowed to enter because he was an Indian. He was hoping to see Teodoro's famous black boots with the flaming red cross or the letter "T", but was not successful, so he went home to await for Don Carlos, Doña Virginia and Luis. On the way he resigned himself to follow Teodoro whenever possible for an opportunity once and for all to ascertain whatever doubt in Luis' mind, for in his own there was not doubt.

As luck would have it, the long awaited confrontation with Teodoro happened in the most unexpected manner when by order of Don Carlos Pepe was guiding a cart drawn by a mule to the brick yard where Pepe was to purchase one hundred bricks for the purpose of repairing part of the kitchen wall. Coming down the main road to that area of the settlement that was slowly developing into the business section, two caballeros galloped almost abreast of Pepe who had not noticed them because he was concentrating all his energy in controlling his recalcitrant mule.

Although there was space enough on the road for one horseman to pass Pepe, the other horseman to follow, something that would have taken possibly a minute or two, the caballeros decided to have some fun with Pepe, who was unknown to them as the son of their victim of fourteen years past. Doroteo charged with his horse causing Pepe to fall in a small canal or ditch that served as drainage to the sporadic rains that dotted the region in the early spring. Pepe got up completely soaked, his clothes full of mud and his temper sorely tempted. Pepe's first thought and desire was to unhorse his tormentor, but the good sense he had learned from his father even at that early age, plus the lessons from his benefactor Don Carlos, and perhaps a little of that submissiveness and timidity instilled in the majority of the descendants of the once proud Aztecs, made him contain himself until the best opportunity for redress presented itself.

When Teodoro fell to the ground, the long awaited question was at answered – there was a "T" on the back of the heels of Teodoro's boots. People had started to gather and if Teodoro had ideas of attacking Pepe with his sword, he had sense enough to realize that this was not the time to punish Pepe because of the many witnesses, to say nothing of Pepe who had taken his machete from the cart and was ready to give a good account of himself. Teodoro put hs sword away, got on his horse and started to trot away not without reminding Pepe that this was an unfinished business which would be resolved at the next opportunity, which he hoped would be soon.

Pepe was not lacking in irony either, and thanking Teodoro for his kind thoughts told him; "Caballero, next Saturday I will be promenading in the back of the edifice that is being used as a church, around midnight, and if by chance you happen to come by, perhaps we will renew acquaintances and, who knows, I may give you a souvenir to remember the occasion." At this, Teodoro reined his horse and visibly furious once more insulted Pepe – "You insolent Indian, how dare you challenge me, a caballero? It would be beneath my dignity to duel with you, and I would not brawl with a peasant, and an Indian at that, with a machete, when we Spaniards settle our differences on the field of honor with the most honorable weapon, our sword. To which Pepe replied, "If settling your differences on the field of honor with your sword is what makes you feel like a gentleman, be advised that I also have a sword, so you should not be going against a peasant with a machete, but against somebody who is itching to teach you a lesson; unless you prefer to run your sword though my back when I am not looking, as I hear someone did that same thing some fourteen years ago to a defenseless man." At this, Teodoro colored visibly and looked at Pepe with a questioning look but recovered sufficiently to tell Pepe, "If it were not for the fact that I will be the laughing stock of this honorable community, I would take you up on your foolish offer which is your death sentence." Pepe had a mordant reply that cut

JOSÉ VALDEZ

Teodoro to the quick, "Your honorable friends and neighbors will really die laughing when word spreads around that you really are trying to hide behind your Spanish birth, and that makes you a coward." When all the people that had gathered started talking to each other, some others were whispering, and the rest were actually smiling and laughing, Teodoro in order to retain some of his pride, addressed Pepe in a furious tone while Pepe remained calm, "Against my better judgment, I will lower myself to accept your challenge because no matter what kind of gossip my action causes, it will be worth it to run my sword through your Aztec heart." The Twins left, Pepe went about his business and the crowd dispersed.

34

Don Carlos Gives Pepe
Valuable Information

Pepe had an idea that Teodoro would accept his challenge so that when it happened he went to Luis to tell him about the duel. Pepe was in a state of exhilaration because somehow luck had placed in his path what in his mind was his father's killer now that he had found out that the marking on Teodoro's boots was a "T". Now, he thought to himself, not only do I have an opportunity to avenge my father, but at the same time I have taken another step in the eyes of the world, toward the goal that he had set out for himself and which had become almost an obsession, equality with the Spaniards. After telling Luis all about the confrontation with Teodoro, both decided that Don Carlos should be apprised of the incident.

JOSÉ VALDEZ

Don Carlos listened intently and looked as if Pepe had proceeded with cool behavior but since encounters such as this needed quite a bit of preparation and planning, Pepe was not to do anything until Don Carlos talked with the Twins. It was still an hour to dark but the Twins had already begun their libations at their favorite tavern when Don Carlos walked in and headed toward the table occupied by Teodoro, Doroteo and their friends.

Spotting Teodoro, Don Carlos approached him and said, "Caballero, it is my understanding that you had some kind of difficulty with my employee, Pepe." Teodoro seemed to have rehearses what he was to reply, "Don Carlos, you may call me by my given name for we know each other well enough, and as what you call a difficulty, there was no such thing but an unprovoked attack on my person by your Indian manservant; and by the way this turn of events is going to prove quite unfortunate for him because I expect redress at the earliest opportunity." Don Carlos wanted to clarify a point, "Since I am vitally interested in this affair, I would like to know what you mean by redress." It was as if Teodoro was expecting to ask for further details when he said, "Your servant, Pepe I believe is his name, had the temerity of challenging me to a clandestine meeting behind the church on Saturday night, where I expect to teach him with sufficient clarity to stay in his place, and to show deference to his betters. If, however, you have come to intercede on his behalf, I am willing to listen provided we begin this discussion with an apology." At this point Don Carlos shed all propriety and in a quite firm and ironical tone replied, "If you expect an apology from Pepe after the foul treatment he received from you and your brother, you are sadly mistaken because from what I hear he expects you will be the one to apologize to him before, during or after the proposed meeting on Saturday night. As it pertains to me, let me advise you that your jokes, for then can not be anything else, will find greater currency on the stage with the rest of your clowns."

When Don Carlos ended his tirade and before Teodoro had anything to reply, Doroteo, full of bravado, joined the heated discussion and directed his remark to Don Carlos, "Sir, you have insulted my brother, and that I will not tolerate without exacting satisfaction in the form of at least an apology from you." At this Don Carlos directed some choice remarks to the other twin, "You, dear sir, are a meddler of the first degree, and as such you will obtain what you deserve, if you care to join our group on Saturday night." Doroteo's reply was in keeping with the challenge received and replied. "I thank you for our courtesy in extending such an invitation which I gladly accept."

Teodoro could not help but condemn his brother's intrusion and said to him, "Doroteo, you fool, you have been maneuvered very nicely, and now you have been compromised."

Following his irresponsible manner of speed Doroteo assured his brother, "Say no more, dear brother, for on Saturday night I will unceremoniously dispatch the high and mighty Don Carlos to the next world before the cleric arrives to give him absolution." Don Carlos had enough of the Twins' impertinence and ended the encounter with the following remark, "I can see that it is useless to talk sensibly to either of you for you two seem devoid of common and

courtesy, which makes me wonder about your upbringing."
Not to be outdone as far as having the last word, Teodoro,
seeing Don Carlos leave, hurled his last tirade, "It seems to
me that you insist on digging your hole deeper and deeper not
realizing that your days of glory are gone, for which reason I
suggest that you put your affairs in order."

35

Pepe and Don Carlos Become Companions-At-Arms

Don Carlos was almost out of the tavern when Teodoro hurled his last bravado so he did not pay any attention to it because he felt quite satisfied at having accomplished his objective that was to maneuver the twins into a confrontation.

Upon arrival at home Don Carlos asked for Pepe and was told that he was working outside supervising the work on the roof of an extension to the kitchen. Pepe was told that Don Carlos wanted to talk to him, and having dropped everything, hurried to Don Carlos' office where he and Luis were already waiting.

Without any preamble, Don Carlos related his meeting with the Twins. He also explained that not through his own choice he was to confront Doroteo and Pepe was to lay host to Teodoro. He went on to explain that since in his opinion Pepe was to confront the more skillful opponent, at this time he was going to do his best to round Pepe's training by teaching him the moves and tricks that through the years had served him in good stead. Don Carlos began by advising Pepe that which every novice should know and never forget no matter what the situation – the success or failure of any plan of attack always depends on plenty of patience, and in connection with this one must be well trained in order to withstand a long siege.

Pepe was overwhelmed with an emotion that he was trying very hard to hide, and all he could do was thank Don Carlos profusely for taking time and interest in his undertaking. In his mind he assessed the situation as another step in his quest for recognition by a Spaniard and he visualized that another Spaniard would look at him differently when he met him on the field of honor Saturday night. He even dared to think that it was as if Don Carlos had chosen to assist in a chivalrous quest; and why not, he asked himself, as he dared to give a greater and more sublime significance to his meeting with Teodoro. Other thoughts came to his mind, all different but all part of his extraordinary situation – he was going to acquit himself as a cavalier would, not only for himself, but also for Don Carlos and Doña Virginia who had been so kind to him, his father and his mother; for Luis who had always shown interest in him and who at this very moment was looking at him in a smiling way that was making him uncomfortable but in a delightful way; and lastly, for his wonderful mother and for his race which, in a way responsible for the attributes that merited his present position.

Attentively, Pepe followed Don Carlos and Luis who was also very much interested in whatever information and/or advice her father was going to impart to Pepe. When they arrived at Don Carlos' private quarters, Don Carlos went to the weapons rack and having chosen a dueling sword to give his words a better effect, asked Luis and Pepe to sit down. Don Carlos began by looking at Pepe and saying, "What I am going to say is more for the benefit of you, Pepe, because all you know about the art of swordsmanship and dueling you have learned in a random manner; and any other time I would not have taken the time to explain certain points because you would have learned them eventually. but this situation requires that you learn them in only a few days."

Don Carlos continued talking to Pepe and Luis who were sitting together and fairly hanging from his every word, "All through the encounter you must be fully poised and ready for action at an instant, with nothing to distract you. Poise and readiness will help you concentrate and will sharpen your powers of observation. Also they will make it easy to take instantaneous action when through your sword you feel the slightest vacillation in your opponent's blade foretelling his next move. Next to keeping your poise is your knowledge of the three most popular and efficacious parries to the most vulnerable areas. For our purposes, I will teach you the best manner to put into effect such maneuvers, but I must warn you that it will be very hard on you because you will have to practice them day and night for we have very little time, and I trust Luis understands all this and does her best to help you.

36

Pepe Learns Strategy From A Master

While at the same time explaining their purpose and when to execute them. "The first parry," he told his audience, "which shall be named as such, has for its purpose to protect the left side of the midriff, and from the lower thorax to the left shoulder. This parry is one of the most used because it is instinctive and protects very easily because your vulnerable area is farther removed from your opponent's weapon considering that you are right handed. This is one parry that you do not have to worry about practicing too much because as I explained it is instinctive, but at the same time you must be on the alert because your opponent may be guessing correctly and that will cause you plenty of trouble."

Continuing his subject Don Carlos described the second move or parry to a more vulnerable area, "The second parry I have perfected by the trial and error system, and I have the marks in my body to show how I learned this defense. This parry serves to protect the opposite side of the area covered by the first but with one exception, your vulnerable area will be closed to your opponent's weapon, for which reason you must spend many of hours in practice. This parry does not have the instinctive quality of the first because this particular area which it will defend will be closer to your adversary, as I said before, and therefore your safety will depend more on your ability and also on your utmost concentration."

Finally, the third parry will protect you from the midriff in the groin, and although it makes its appearance in a match only about fifteen to twenty percent of the time, you must always expect an attack to this area because failure to respond in a proper manner could be quite dangerous. The reason why this defense against this particular lunge or thrust comprises such a small percentage of a plan of attack and defense is because the blade is held at eyesight level, and the necessary degree of deviation of your opponent's hand, wrist and arm bears a forewarning quality besides being awkward in comparison to the other forms of attack and defense."

In closing his talk Don Carlos gave one last piece of valuable advice, "Now I will tell you about the tactics that I have used with a good deal of success. The key words to this very simple plan of defense are patience, perseverance and poise. Keeping in mind that a feint should be made with arm and wrist only, choose any kind of maneuver that you can initiate and repeat constantly every time your adversary is in a feint or "en garde" position. The kind of maneuver that you use should be one that you can perform with ease and fluidity, and its purpose is to lull your adversary into a sense of security which will appear when he starts thinking that he knows what your next move will be. As is well known, man is a creature of habit from where comfort and ease is derived as well as relief from the unexpected; and all one has to do is wait for the opening which is bound to come. This is all I have to tell you, except that I do not worry about the outcome because you have three big advantages in your favor – youth, strength and purpose."

The news spread fast throughout "La Morada" of the impending confrontation, and the special police detachment which had been operating under the auspices of the Oficina Central de Seguridad of Mexico City found itself in a quandary as to how to proceed because on the one hand the contingent was supposed to keep the peace, and Captain Julio Montes could not figure out whether such an undertaking as stopping a duel came under his authority, since La Morada had not been granted a charter; and duels could not be forbidden, as they were in Mexico City. On the other hand, Captain Montes, in sizing up the situation, had mixed thoughts about the principals in the confrontation. Don Carlos, he reasoned correctly, will surely dispose of Doroteo, a good friend of his, and that worried him; and as far as Teodoro was concerned, also a very good friend, he did ot worry because he had shown in previous experiences that he was a better than average swordsman who could take care of himself although in some instances he had not settled the issue unscathed.

37

Doña Manuela Pleads For Doroteo And Don Carlos And Pepe Find Seconds For Their Match

Other personages in the developing drama who were very much interested in the outcome were Doña Manuela and Don Felipe. After talking to her brothers and understanding the situation with all probabilities, she went to her husband for advice and comfort. After listening to the story, slanted to her view and the Twins, Don Felipe told his wife that the only way for Teodoro and Doroteo to extricate themselves from the mess they had created was to render their opponents a complete apology on the field of honor.

This brought a spirited retort from Manuela, "I did not expect such crude and heartless words from you, Felipe; don't you realize that we are in the middle of a different situation which will have serious repercussions if this duel takes place?" Don Felipe's answer cut Manuela to the quick, "I see only that two Spanish Caballeros do not see eye to eye on some point of view and having exhausted their arguments have mutually decided to let their swords settle the dispute on the field of honor, which is the manner in which problems of this type have been resolved for generations." Doña Manuela was not convinced, "Felipe, all I am asking is that you intercede with Don Carlos to go easy on my brother, Doroteo, for it is my understanding that Don Carlos is quite superior to Doroteo in swordsmanship, and as far as Teodoro is concerned, he will take good care of that upstart indian."

With an air of finality, Don Felipe replied, "If I were to do that, which is demeaning in its nature to me as well as to your brother would make me laughing stock. However, and trying to be of some help, let me explain that in a woman the mother complex reigns and is considered a most natural task, so why don't you go see Don Carlos yourself and plead your case."

As her husband suggested, Manuela went to Don Carlos' home and having found him and Doña Virginia, after a few niceties, came straight to the point, "Don Carlos, are you going through with this unequal contest? You don't have to, you know, because it is an accepted fact that you don't have to prove anything." To which Don Carlos replied, "Señora, if the King, himself, asked me I would refuse." One last argument remained for Doña Manuela, "Don Carlos, will you please spare his ignorance and just teach him a lesson?" Don Carlos was finding it very difficult to carry on this type of conversation and told her, "Señora, it is quite obvious that you don't realize what you are asking of me because if somehow, to please you, I do something contrary to my system of manner of execution, I may invite disaster if my opponent is smart enough to sense weakness, and try to take advantage of the situation." As a parting shot Doña Manuela said as she walked out, " I will be praying that you understand the possible consequences of this confrontation."

Don Carlos and Doña Virginia tried to guess if there was a hidden meaning to Doña Manuela's words, but Don Carlos gave up and told his wife that Doña Manuela was overwrought and had nothing else to say; and besides he had no choice to abide by the code of chivalry.

Knowing that there was very little time in which to get organized, Don Carlos had his horse saddled and rode to Doctor Enrique Bragelone's office, and luckily found him as he was leaving, presumably to his estate for a siesta as the custom was all around after the noonday repast.

Don Carlos explained to his friend the situation that had developed. He then told Doctor Bragelone the reason for his visit to the Doctor, "Don Enrique, even though I have many friends that could help, I have decided to ask you to be my second." "Of course, Don Carlos," Don Enrique replied, "on this or any other situation you can count on me." "Thank you, Don Enrique, I knew that I could count on you, and now, I am asking another favor, do you know of anybody that may favor my man, Pepe, who I consider a very good friend, by representing him?" Don Enrique thought for a moment, "The situation being what it is, all of us can understand that it would entail a little bit of difficulty finding a Spanish Caballero to act as Pepe's "padrino" because of his Aztec

JOSÉ VALDEZ

descent, but we are in luck for my younger brother, Ruben, twenty-nine years old and a pretty good swordsman in his own right would love to take part in this drama, and I can vouch for his presence as requested."

Before leaving, elated that his mission had been a success, Don Carlos added a little piece of advice, "From my experience and other data, all of us may be in more than a simple duel, so we should keep an eye open for any eventuality." "Don Carlos," Don Enrique assured him, "We will be ready for anything, and it is high time we had something around La Morada to make life a little bit interesting." With that the friends parted, as Ruben arrived. Don Enrique explained to his brother what was expected of him and as he had surmised, Ruben was all for fulfilling his duty as "padrino, " and hoping things would turn out just right for him to get into the action himself.

38

Don Carlos and Pepe Get Ready For Action And Doña Virginia and Luisa Disclose Secrets To Each Other

Don Carlos seemed like a new man and Doña Virginia could not be happier to see him act as if he were in his twenties; full of vigor and energy and a clear and happy countenance. Nevertheless, she felt a certain amount of misgiving that she realized was the natural feeling of a wife whose husband was going to face danger. Nothing like that bothered Don Carlos who felt the exhilaration and excitement of impending action just as he used to experience before going into battle. He would walk with a brisk step, talk ot the servants he met on his way with a cheerful accent, take a look at Pepe's practice and talk at length with his daughter, who cold not help but betray emotion for her childhood friend and companion, Pepe.

JOSÉ VALDEZ

Early Saturday morning, the day of confrontation, Don Carlos gave the final touches to the lessons his companion-at-arms had been practicing and helped him choose a dueling sword. Pepe was beside himself because of all the attention he was receiving from no less than the famous Don Carlos, who having been one of Don Hernan Cortés' greatest paladins, was now treating him in a manner which he could not have expected in his wildest dreams.

In his mind, and with good reason, he would ponder at the goal he had set out to accomplish, which was to strive for the equality that was the heritage of his forebearers before they were beaten into submission, and he felt satisfaction. These thoughts would give way at times when he even dared to look at Luis trying to read in her eyes any feeling that would tell him that there was in them something more than good friendship but the years of servitude had forced him to act servile and also instilled in his mind an attitude which prevented him from seeing in her eyes a recurrent flash or sparkle, ever so dim, that betrayed feelings which she had finally understood and accepted.

Late in the afternoon all three accompanied Doña Virginia in a light snack on the advice of Don Carlos who explained the reason for a light repast; and after a lengthy conversation, mostly about family matters, during which Pepe did not and could not participate except when the topic veered to repairs of the buildings and general husbandry, the time arrived for Don Carlos and Pepe to mount their horses and be on their way, promptness being one of the qualities of a true caballero, he explained.

After they had left, Doña Virginia and Luisa engaged in a very interesting conversation. Luisa was fifteen and with an understanding of life far beyond her years, for after all, she was an uncommon person which leading a double life, gave the two different vantage points from which to observe life. "Luis," Doña Virginia began, using the masculine form of Luisa which she never used when they were alone, "I think I know what your feelings are at this moment because more or less I am in the situation." Luis answered, "Mamá, it was almost until they left that I finally realized what my feelings are toward Pepe; and what a terrible blow it would be for me if something should happen to him."

Doña Virginia decided to tell her daughter her great secret at this time, "Luisa," she began in the natural appellation, "I understand your feelings which more and more have become noticeable, and whatever course of action you follow in this particular matter, I approve your choice. Also, naturally, I can feel misgiving about your father as you about Pepe, and if, as I surmise your feelings are such that you would prefer to take Pepe's place, let me tell you something that will tell you and I have those same feelings," Doña Virginia continued after a short pause during which Luisa started wondering what her mother was going to disclose. "In my day, I was just as anxious to learn about swords when I read about the famous Russian Countess Wasilika who, passed for a man before the fact was revealed that she was a woman, faced in her life., in the court of the Czar seven adversaries and was victorious in all of them, three of her adversaries having died from wounds received. So taken was I with the Countess Wasilika's prowess and heroic deeds spread all over Europe, that I asked my father to teach me swordsmanship; but he refused, my uncle Raul Bragelone, who was considered a pretty good swordsman in his day, made a fair sword-wielding lady out of me."

Doña Virginia continued while Luis looked at her with wonder and surprise, "From what I have seen, you are pretty good, plus you have stamina, something that I lack at this moment but in a given situation or emergency, I am quite sure, because of my experience, that I can give a good account of myself. As you can see, I understand your feelings about what is going on tonight, but I don't think there is anything we can do but wait. "Mamá," Luis said, "I don't think I can stand the uncertainty so I have a good mind to go although I dare not go by myself.

39

Doña Virginia And Luis Attend As Uninvited Guests, As Doroteo Learns A Costly Lesson

Doña Virginia took advantage of the hint and told Luis, "I knew you would eventually decide to go, and to that effort I had a coach ready even before you talked about going because as I said, I am in the same situation and uncertainty, so let us go." Antonio, the stable boy, came to announce that the coach was ready, and mother and daughter boarded it after Doña Virginia dressed for the occasion with a tight fitting garment, while Luis, as always, wore pants.

When they arrived, Antonio stationed the coach at the edge of a portico that covered the entrance to a side door leading to the sacristy of the church; and as luck would have it, next to the horses of Don Carlos, Pepe and their seconds, the brothers

Bragelone. From their vantage point behind the columns of the portico they could observe clearly enough the proceedings due to the fact that there was a bright moon; and being behind the columns of the portico, they could not be seen.

They had arrived almost to the end of the preliminary talks leading to acceptance of rules on both sides; and were not aware that the seconds of Don Carlos and Pepe had been unsuccessful in their proposal to change the format of two single duels into a two against two, no holds barred, first blood participant to have a choice of continuing or yielding, the remaining member also allowed to have the same choice. The Twins declined for reasons of their own, and the first duel was ruled to be Doroteo against Don Carlos, which began without any preamble except the required "en garde" command.

Doroteo, not having had much experience in situation of this type exposed his naiveté by attacking as if he were to gain a quick victory, instead of trying to feel the enemy for the purpose of defining his method of play. Doroteo's bumbling and haphazard ways assured Don Carlos that he could end this farce any time he wanted; which he did by a quick flourish which jolted the sword from Doroteo's hand, at practically the same time that his own sword found a soft spot on Doroteo's lower left thorax, which area started to bleed profusely.

As soon as Don Carlos disengaged his weapon, the duel was declared officially over as the amount of blood could not be contained. Doroteo's "padrino" laid him on the grass and took care of the wound that was not judged to be critical, and as soon as possible was taken to Doña Manuela's estancia.

The notice having been given, the next two contestants were admonished to be en garde, an advice that in Pepe's case was inutile and unnecessary because he was raring to do, for the moment he had been waiting for was there. He was not thinking about the fact that he could be killed or permanently maimed because being there was enough to obliterate any other thoughts. Being there in what the Spaniards referred to as the field of honor, measuring his skill against a Spaniard Caballero, even if that person was one of the worst, was something he had always anticipated and dreamed about ever since he had started handling a sword. Best of all, he reasoned, for his encounter served many purposes, he was there and for that he thanked the Lord not only for himself but also for his race who in a mall way would regain some of the pride that was lost when the princess "La Malinche" threw her lot with Don Hernan Cortés, and because of her contribution in translating had a hand in the defeat and subjugation of her own people.

The match went as Don Carlos expected and was proud of Pepe who was following all his advice and instruction, "Keep your concentration and poise, let him think he has the upper hand; make him work so that his wrist begins to feel the strain; you are young and with plenty of stamina while he has squandered all of his strength in the local cantinas; and be sure to remember that you have in reserve our left arm which is something that he does not know or expect; and most important be on the alert because if he feels getting tired he will throw everything in one last desperate gamble and that will be his most dangerous move." Such were the thoughts racing through the mind of Don Carlos.

JOSÉ VALDEZ

40

Pepe Claims A Double Victory

As if somehow Don Carlos could communicate his thoughts, Pepe was doing exactly that. Pepe was exchanging force with force, subtlety with subtlety, craftiness with method and appropriate response, always on the alert for feints, and always parrying every thrust or lunge of Teodoro, but never attacking. This type of action began to bother Teodoro who began to have second thoughts about handling an adversary who had never held a sword in a situation like the present a young Indian at that. He began to make little mistakes in his delivery, and when he felt that his wrist began to tire a little, he realized that attrition was necessarily his forte.

Teodoro started to force the issue more and more, and the fact that his plan brought him some success when he inflicted two slight wounds on Pepe's dueling arm made him think that he was finally breaking through the indian's defense. This assumption could not have been more wrong because all of a sudden Pepe became a veritable whirlwind, who completely neutralized every move of his opponent to a point that quite easily he began to inflict wounds and cuts to Teodoro in the areas of the thorax, arm and left side of the chest. Teodoro, in one final surge lunged to the chest but Pepe, having complete mastery of the field, evaded his move adroitly, and making his adversary pay for his mistake, felt his sword slide through Teodoro's abdomen almost to the hilt, which dropped him in a pool of blood which his seconds tried to contain as much as they could as they carried him to the coach.

Pepe stood motionless bleeding from various wounds, his body feeling no pain, but his mind was trying to place in perspective the various thoughts that engulfed him. He did not feel exultation as the victor in a match where the consensus had assigned him the role of underdog. He felt that only a sense of relief at having accomplished something that had taken many years – revenge on one of the assassins of his father, and a Spaniard Caballero, at that. He also felt pride at having proven to himself that the Spaniard was not invincible, and, he said to himself, it is only a matter of time before others will follow in my footsteps and our race will once more regain some respect.

He was still in a sort of reverie when he heard the voice of Don Carlos, "Pepe, my boy, are you all right?" Abruptly he realized that he was supposed to answer Don Carlos,

JOSÉ VALDEZ

Enrique and Ruben, "Yes, Don Carlos, I feel fine." The Bragelone brothers were congratulating him and he did not know what to say. At that moment another surprise left the four swordsmen speechless when Doña Virginia and Luis came into the open. For one split second all four took their weapons in one hand and were ready for action until they recognized Doña Virginia and Luis, two svelte figures in the moonlight. Don Carlos was embraced by his wife, who then proceeded to embrace Pepe, also ; Luis embraced his father and Pepe. The Bragelone brothers were greeted too and excitement reigned all around, and Don Carlos, regaining some composure, "Virginia and Luis, what are you doing here, and why did you come?" Doña Virginia answered with the most plausible answer she could muster at the moment, "We were worried about both of you." To which Luis added, "We could not just wait, not knowing."

When all this was going on, Pepe thought that he must be dreaming for how else could he explain to himself that Don Carlos had expressed that he cared for him; that Doña Virginia acted as affectionate; that even Luis had embraced him in such a way that his nearness revealed to him a sentiment so ecstatic that anything close to it had never felt in his life, and he was sure that it just had to be a dream.

41

Luis Explains To Her Father Why
She Was There, There Is No Fury
Like That Of A Woman Scorned

Don Carlos thought for a moment about what his wife and Luis had said, and looking fixedly at them offered an alternative reason for their presence, "Of course I can understand your reason for wanting to be here but, since discussion at home had it that I was not going to be in any danger because of the inexperience of my adversary, a thought is nagging my mind that maybe there was a stronger reason, would you say I am right, Luis?" The query having been directed at him, Luis was taken aback momentarily but recovered and answered with a number of explanation, "Father, if you refer to Pepe's encounter, yes, we, (not I) were concerned about him first because he was going against a

Spanish Caballero with plenty of experience in matters such as the present one; secondly, Pepe, with all that he learned from the Master of Arms through the lessons I attended, and all he learned from you, he was still considered the underdog. Finally if it had not been for you, and I do accept a little of the blame, he would not have been in a sort of double-edged sword – the position that I know he relished to avenge his father, while at the same time having to contend with the uncertainty and consequences of putting his life on the line." "That is true, Luis," admitted Don Carlos and the Bragelone brothers agreed. Without any more to do after taking care of Pepe's wounds, the Bragelone brothers departed after receiving thanks from everybody, and the family of Don Carlos, including Pepe also went home where Juana was waiting for her son, Pepe. Embracing and joy ensued all around, and Pepe and Luis looked at one another and smiled.

The two wounded brothers were taken to Doña Manuela's house where a doctor, Alberto Mendez, who had been summoned by her as a precautionary measure, ascertained that Doroteo's wound was not critical and he would be up and around in a week; however, Doctor Mendez added, he should rest as much as possible; and as concerned Teodoro, he was lucky that no vital organs had been damaged, but his recovery would take at least a month to a month and a half because of the amount of blood he had lost.

Ever since Doroteo was brought to her on a stretcher, she had been beside herself with anger, but changed into fury when Teodoro was also brought in badly wounded. She was so furious that her features seemed to be distorted as she cast threats, curses and all sort of damnations directed at the persons who had perpetrated such treatment to her brothers. Her eyes, the most expressible part of her face would almost close to a slit intermittently and upon opening them seemed to exude fire. The time will come, she swore, when all will be repaid and revenge will be very sweet. The seconds of the Twins, who were witnessing her tirades, could only look at each other and wonder what they would feel or do to counteract the bitter hate exhibited by Doña Manuela had they been the object of her fury.

Doctor Alberto Mendez left, promising to return the next day to check on his patients; and Doña Manuela thanked him and also thanked the seconds who had remained, as part of their commitment, to ascertain the condition of the Twins, should this information be required for any purpose, legal or otherwise, Doña Manuela also took the names of the seconds for she planned to contact them in the future. Toton, Tamon and Lardon, were all brothers and members of the Palmas family, and also members of the clique or gang controlled by the Twins, which fact Doña Manuela ignored.

42

Don Carlos Uses Deception, Luis Finds A Brother

The best care that Doña Manuela could dispense, good healthy meals and healing indian potions and herbs worked wonders for the Twins; especially the indian remedies that Doctor Mendez decided to use, at the instigation of an indian "curandero" (healer), because there was scarcity of regular drugs. The combination of those factors brought health to Doña Manuela's brothers, but not to their disposition which made them spend most of their time hurling all types of threats, abominations and dire acts of vengeance.

The result of the confrontation between members of the two families, (Pepe was practically considered a member of the family of Don Carlos), caused a serious distancing and very close to an outright break in their relationship. However, in a forgiving mood, Don Carlos tried to feel the general state of the devious, a talk with his wife convinced everybody that a little furtive endeavor could be useful in this situation.

Antonio, the stable boy, who already had been a witness to the affairs of honor and consequently gained some stature, was called by Don Carlos and Doña Virginia to be briefed on what to do when he visited Don Felipe's estancia. Antonio was supposed to gather information of the condition of the Twins and the general atmosphere around Doña Manuela and Don Felipe. The task assigned to Antonio did not offer him any undue difficulties because for quite some time he had been carrying an amorous relationship with one of the young girls working in Doña Manuela's mansion, a mestiza by the name of Lucia Mata, the couple meeting regularly in a place in the woods nearby.

Antonio assured Don Carlos that since he was to see Lucia that very night, he was sure he would have some news the next morning. Promptly around 7:00 pm, after he had settled the horses and other stock in the stables for the night, and had a big supper at Juana's kitchen, Antonio started across the fields on his way to his loving Lucia who was already waiting for him at their usual place in the woods, close to Doña Manuela's mansion.

While Antonio went on his mission, Don Carlos called a meeting of the family for a discussion of two very important issues that stemmed from the recent developments that had affected the two families. When Pepe was told that he was to attend the meeting also, he stood bewildered and could not obey the summons because he was not sure that he had heard correctly. However, Don Carlos again asked him to join in the meeting because he was to be one of the subjects to be one of the subjects discussed.

Don Carlos spoke first, "Because of these unfortunate incidents, it has become necessary either to amend the contract with Don Felipe's family, or to abrogate it in its entirety by legal means." Doña Virginia reminded her husband, "We do not have a reason strong enough to warrant such action." Don Carlos told her, "Doña Virginia, if having put two members of Don Felipe's relatives out of commission does not constitute an untenable situation, I do not know to what lengths we must go to create one, especially when we are all aware of the explosive character of Doña Manuela; and the worst that can result is forfeiture of the sum of money agreed upon, according to the last item of the contract, a sum of money which we can easily afford."

Doña Virginia must have had something in mind when she asked the following, "If the contract is dissolved, does that mean that Luis can pursue her other life? As a young lady?' Don Carlos answered, "I do not think it is wise for Luis to do that just yet because our action in abrogating the contract might be misinterpreted, that is, it could be considered a subterfuge. So with in mind, as we have already discussed, let us bring Pepe into this discussion by asking his opinion on a very important subject."

Pepe was in a sort of reverie when Don Carlos called "Pepe." Having collected his wits Pepe said, ""Don Carlos, whatever your wish I will be glad to comply, for I care very much for you and Doña Virginia, and I would welcome every opportunity to repay all that you have done for my father, my mother and me." Don Carlos replied, "Pepe, through the years we have seen you develop into the type of young man anybody would be proud to have as a son. Partly because of our debt to your father who was killed while protecting our interests, and partly because looking into the future there will have to be someone to perpetuate our family name, we, my wife and I, would like to have you come into our family as an adopted son."

43

Luisa Accepts Her New Brother And Doña Manuela Draws Plans For Vengeance

Don continued, "Sorry we have not brought you into this before, but that was because we were sure you would not have any objections, do you, Luis?" Luis replied, "I would be lying if I did not admit that this comes as a surprise; a pleasant surprise, at that, because ever since I was a little girl, I have always looked at Pepe as a sort of older brother; and later, as a very dear friend, so I welcome your decision for up to now I have always considered Pepe as part of my family."

Don Carlos then spoke to Pepe, "What do you say, Pepe? If you agree, for the present you will keep your family's surname that you inherited from your father and will be known as Jose Montero. For obvious reasons, at this time you can not carry our family's name, which eventually we will ask you to accept." At this, visibly affected by the offer Don Carlos had made replied, "I am overwhelmed, Don Carlos, and I would like all to know that although I am very proud of my father's legacy, when the time comes I will do as you wish and I will bring nothing but honor to your name. Doña Virginia showed her enthusiasm when she told Pepe, "Dear Pepe, we expect great things from you, and all of us are very happy to welcome you as a member of our family. My husband tells me that official recognition will not be long in coming as soon as the Bragelone brothers deliver the official request some time in the next day or so."

Thanking everybody again, Pepe asked to be excused and ran to tell his mother what had happened. Juana was overjoyed and thanked God for showering so many favors on Pepe and on her.

On the following morning, around 7:00 am Antonio burst into the nook on the veranda which was the place Don Carlos preferred for his breakfast, where at this time the family had a new guest, Pepe, who seemed awkward and with an embarrassed mien, while Juana, her face showing an impish grin at her son's discomfiture, catered to everyone's needs.

Don Carlos, realizing that there was another visitor admonished Antonio, "Take your time, calm yourself and let us know what you have found out." Antonio told him, "Ay, Don Carlos, I kept asking Lucia to repeat what she had told me and she kept telling me the same thing, and it is a terrible thing." Don Carlos repeated, "Confound it, Antonio! Tell us what Lucia told you that you think is so terrible." Antonio finally got his wits together and said, "Doña Manuela had the

Twins sitting on chairs for they felt up to it, and also present was Doctor Alberto Mendez and the three Palmas brothers, these last would just as soon kill you as look at you, but Don Felipe was not present."

"Doña Manuela had a meeting in a chamber far removed from the main drawing room and other alcoves because she did not want Don Felipe to know what she was going to say. That chamber, by the way is contiguous to the little bedroom assigned to Lucia and that is the reason that she found out all that transpired at the meeting." Don Carlos asked Antonio to continue which he did, "It seems that Doña Manuela and her followers are planning to do a lot of damage to your livestock and property; and if the occasion presents itself, to you also, and with special attention given to finding a way to dispose of Pepe, who as an indian had the audacity to think of himself as an equal to her own brothers."

"But when is all this to happen, Antonio?" Antonio answered, "Lucia told me that Doña Manuela tentatively set the date for November 2, which is All Souls Day, because the celebration would help cover their actions. If all goes well, " she added, I will get a little bit of that revenge that I desire which will make me very happy, and everyone will be handsomely rewarded." She ended the meeting by swearing everyone to secrecy and cautioned everybody to attend tomorrow night's meeting for the final plans."

Don Carlos slapped Antonio on the back and said to him, "Well done, Antonio, if we can find out what the final plans are, you will have your own horse and there will be a little gift of appreciation from us to your girlfriend, Lucia. You have served us well and we will do what we can for you." Antonio left promising to return as soon as more information is elicited from Lucia. Knowing that more than likely the date of the raid would be on All Souls Day, gave Don Carlos and all his family time enough to prepare a welcome party, which was really going to be a surprise party.

JOSÉ VALDEZ

44

Officially, Pepe Becomes A Family Member And Antonio Brings Detailed Plans Of Raid to Don Carlos

Don Carlos was all business, "Virginia, bring in all documents pertaining to the members of the 'encomienda' so that we can amend the one belonging to Pepe so that we can draw a petition for change in family kinship which both of us and Pepe, as Jose Montero will sign. Don Ruben Bragelone, as licensed barrister in Spain and in New Spain will notarize such document. Pepe, run over to Don Ruben and ask him to come and exercise his offices, after which you will ride to Mexico City to file our petition in the archives covering our family history."

Doña Virginia, in a light hearted, fun-loving mood, spoke to Luis, "Looks like we will have a chance to exercise our talents, after all." To which Luis replied, "Mamá, I can hardly wait for the action to begin for I also want to show that we, the Monsibais de la Fosa family know how to deal with this shady element and will make them pay dearly for their temerity."

Since everyone had chores to do, Don Carlos was left alone, which he did not mind because all he wanted was wait for Antonio and whatever news he had obtained from Lucia. It was vital to find out if Doña Manuela had finally decided on the second day of November, All Souls Day, was the target day for her deed. All day long Don Carlos waited to hear from Antonio but Antonio met Lucia very late at night, so he had to wait until the next day to tell Don Carlos of the definite plans for the aggression.

In the meantime, since he started on his trip to Mexico City on the thirtieth day of October, late in the afternoon, at the behest of Don Carlos, Pepe traveled the 140 kilometers to the capital arriving there on the last day of October. After discharging his duties, he started on his way back to La Morada, and arrived at Don Carlos' hacienda on the first day of November, before Old Saints Day, having hardly slept in two days, but happy to be in possession of the precious document. Immediately, he went to the private office where, as luck would have it, Antonio was about to narrate to Don Carlos the plans that Doña Manuela had laid to her followers.

Pepe took a seat next to Luis and Doña Virginia, and all stood very quiet in order not to miss a single word of Antonio's information. Antonio began by telling them that according to what Lucia heard the Pelma brothers, Toton,

Tamon and Lardon were slated to do as much damage as they could by gaining entry through the lowest part of the adobe wall anchored to which, was the gate that allowed only enough space at its base for the water from the stream to flow into the compound in order to fill the pool and water the grass, fruit trees and flower gardens. While the Pelma brothers were operating at the gate, the shady Doctor Mendez and the Twins, Teodoro and Doroteo plus a few malefactors that these last would recruit, were assigned to open the pens in the corrales to stampede the cattle and other stock, which maneuver would make it easy to rustle a few head.

With this information Don Carlos saw his way clear to map his own strategy to counteract the proposed raid on his hacienda. Subject to the approval and understanding of everybody, including the Bragelone brothers who were also to be present on this religious holiday, All Saints Day, his plan was as follows: "I do not claim to have all the answers," he said to all, "so I welcome any suggestion form one. We have taken away from these brigands the element of surprise, which factor is in our favor.

The way I see it, according to Antonio's report, we will probably see action on three places – at the water gate for possible entrance to the house, in the pens and corrales, and in the stables close to the main postern. Since the Twins and Doctor Mendez are going to concentrate their questionable activities to the pens in the buildings next to the large corrales, it is obvious that they picked this area because they do not want to run the risk of being recognized."

45

Preparations Are Made On All Saints Day And On All Saints Day, The Hacienda Rocks With Celebration

Don Carlos, then, directed his words to the Bragelone brothers, I extend an invitation to you Enrique, and to you, Ruben, to join me, my family and a few trusted indians in welcoming these brigands in a most proper manner, and in doing so, to send them to the infirmary and other worse places." Don Enrique answered, "Don Carlos, I know I am speaking also for my brother Ruben when we accept this invitation and thank you for this opportunity to rid society of some of these outlaws."

Just then Pepe asked Don Carlos, "What about me? I would like to be with you when you meet the Twins because I want to finish the job that I set out to do, and did not." Don Carlos replied, "Pepe, you will have to wait for another opportunity because in my opinion this is not a matter of choosing where to fight, but where the person will be more effective in the overall scheme. It is expected that with the speed that you and Luis have, plus the steadying influence of Doña Virginia, and the courage of Juana and the rest of the household crew, the three bumbling malefactors, Toton, Tamon and Lardon and their gang will soon be taken care of because they will no doubt be under the influence of wine and pulque expecting an easy job. As soon as you dispatch them, the two of you should either help Antonio and his indians at the stables, or come to help us clean up the gang attacking the corrales."

During the rest of the day, which was All Saints Day, all personnel in the household went about their business as if there were not a care in the world, getting everything ready for the next day, All Souls Day afternoon and night celebration, for the morning was to be dedicated to remembrance of the departed with a Mass and special prayers and benediction. A frugal repast was to complete the traditional All Souls Day morning tribute to the dearly departed.

In the afternoon of All Souls Day everybody wore the mask each had been working on for days, and since everyone had been very secretive, there were plenty of surprises, laughter and plenty of fun. There were two big and extra long tables full of kinds of viands, meats, fruits and candy. One of these tables was set on the patio just outside the glass door leading to the study where Don Carlos spent many hours writing his memoirs; the other table also lavish with food, meat and fruits was set in the family's private dining room which on this day was open to all personnel.

Hours passed and about 8:00 pm the "piece of resistance" was announced. This part of the program, although awaited by everyone, was mainly for the enjoyment of the children. The main character in this act had to do with a sort of pantomime, a person with a mask purporting to be the face of Judas Iscariote. This person did not volunteer for this role, nor was chosen by anybody, but to his discomfiture had drawn the black ball.

Judas was to put on his mask, dress in rags and in general tried to look as horrible and mean as possible so that the smaller children would be frightened. The little children would cry and try to hide in the flowing skirts of their mothers, and all would laugh and possibly recollect memories of their distant past when they were also afraid of Judas. However, the older kids, who obviously had already participated in the celebration for at least one previous year, would act as if they were actually afraid of the person purporting to be Judas, but as soon as he would turn around, they would give him a good whack on his rump with a stick hidden behind their back, which action being or not being part of the program would however, smart enough to make Judas try to catch the perpetrator to retaliate by dispensing alike or more punishment as the real Judas would have probably administered under the same circumstances.

While all this fun and merriment was going on, Don Carlos and his chosen allies stealthily left the fiesta in order to take the posts most likely to be attacked, because it was to be expected that the assault would not be long in coming.

JOSÉ VALDEZ

46

Pandemonium At the Water Gate, Juana Gives A Good Account Of Herself

Little by little everybody started to show signs of fatigue which was to be expected after the entire day's celebration; and even the children did not find Judas interesting any more, nor the food and sweets on the tables appealing, having had their fill of everything.

As if by a prearranged signal around 9:00 pm the crowd dispersing except the chosen few that previously had been assigned the different posts headed by Doña Virginia with Pepe and Luis at the gate area where they lay in wait behind two stately trees which stood one on each side of the gate; by Don Calos with the Bragelone brothers, Enrique and Ruben, at the pens and corrales; and Antonio at the stables where he was having his hands full trying to keep his indians in check for they ere becoming unruly because they were raring to go into action.

Doña Manuela's plan was to send her terrible trio of ruffians, Toton, Lardon and Tamon over to the gate to create confusion as a diversionary tactic, so that the Twins, Teodoro and Doroteo might have an easier time dispersing and stampeding the cattle. The main purpose of this maneuver was to rustle as many head as possible for she reasoned that by hitting Don Carlos at his pocketbook often enough he was bound to feel the pinch, and she would get some vengeance, and also, dividends for the gang.

What Doña Manuela did not bargain for was that the so called terrible trio would remain sober until the raid was accomplished because they were under the influence of pulque when they started because they figured that it was going to be an easy undertaking. The trio gained to the top of the water gate, and not having enough balance fell in a heap on the inside of the gate, and their four of five followers not seeing them, jumped over, too, and landed on Toton and Lardon causing them to emit groans of pain accompanied by the usual cursing which clamor could not help but he heard within at least a fifty foot radius, so there went their stealthy approach.

To all intents and purposes, the two malefactors, Toton and Lardon were put out of commission but not our of their misery because Toton suffered a broken leg and Lardon a couple of ribs. At that time, a prearranged whistle was heard which Doña Virginia interpreted to be the signal for attack, which began when Tamon, the only one of the trio

JOSÉ VALDEZ

still standing, was engaged by Doña Virgina. Pepe and Luis, meanwhile were not idle at all, and each engaged and dispatched promptly one of the trio's aides leaving only two of the original crew, as the fifth one found in the darkness the gate which he had no trouble in negotiating. Due to the darkness Tamon could only surmise that things were not going well for the group hearing the moans, groans and curses of his brothers, Toton and Lardon, and when he guessed that two of the four remaining members of the crew had been dispatched by Pepe and Luis, he started to withdraw toward the gate but Doña Virginia was not to be denied.

She pressed him and when Tamon tried to look for the gate, something Doña Virginia did not have to do because she knew the terrain well, he lost his concentration and was run through the upper leg close to the groin which caused him to fall in a heap. Even though the wound was serious and disabling, what for the moment hurt him the most was the fact that he considered himself quite a swordsman, and was finding out that he had been bested by a woman when Doña Virginia asked him to yield or be killed.

Doña Virginia then turned her attention to the two brigands that she thought were still left but was reassured by Pepe and Luis that while they were taking the measure of two of the four, Juana had managed to slip behind them and deftly wielded an oversized cast iron skillet with which she smashed the skull of one, while the other one, who had turned around to attack her, felt the same skillet disfigure his face forever, and fell in a dead heap to the ground bleeding from cuts and lacerations all over his face and forehead.

47

Outcome At Pens, Corrales And Stables

All of the wounded attackers on the home front having been secured, awaiting to be turned over to the proper authorities, Pepe and Luis ran to the pens to bolster the defensive group made up of Don Carlos, the Bragelone brothers and some servants, but were told the situation was well in hand.

The only thing that remained unsolved was Antonio and his indians at the stables, and the Bragelone brothers offered to go with Don Carlos' consent, to help clean up the rest of the raiding hoodlums. That gave Don Carlos a little time to tell what had happened to Doña Virginia, Luis and Pepe. "As soon as the din of sword play was heard," Don Carlos began, "as if by previous design, Doctor Mendez and the Twins rode all the way to the pens and corrales, followed by some of their friends and dismounted as if they were going to perform some simple task or going to a fiesta, since the celebration or any kind of ritual pertaining to All Souls Day still had some time to go before midnight."

Don Carlos concluded, "Doña Manuela's program could not have been better for us even if they had rehearsed the plot. In a way we have to give credit to Doña Manuela or the Twins for having sent those bunglers as vanguards, playing it safe just in case, but those same bunglers completely destroyed the element of surprise which they thought they had, not knowing that there was not going to be any surprised, obviously. When they started hearing moans, groans and yells which they judged correctly as originating from their own forces, the Twins became completely demoralized when we jumped them and disposed promptly of three or four of their men in the first few minutes, while the others, who apparently from the beginning were not too sure this was their affair, made good use of their legs and got away in the dark."

"That left the twins who were engaged by Enrique and Ruben while I happened to find Doctor Mendez in time to explain to him that handling a sword is not quite the same as brandishing a scalpel on some poor soul who can not retaliate. After I gave him a few scratches for I did not want to do him much harm because I was sure that he had been duped and used by the Twins, he yielded and disclosed his name, after which I let him go."

While this little episode was taking place, the Bragelone brothers were having a grand old time with Teodoro and Doroteso, who not being on a par with Enrique and Ruben partly because of their recent embarrassment which put them in bed for a couple of weeks, and partly because they felt they had been caught like little kids swiping candy from the proverbial jar, were having a most difficult time trying to evade serious damage, at the same time that they were retreating to where their horses had been tethered.

In the dark, although keeping from revealing their identity, Teodoro could not help shouting, "Mendez, where are you going, you coward." Upon hearing that voice Don Carlos shouted, "I would know our voice anywhere, Teodoro, and I knew it had to be you and your no-good twin." No answer from either of the Twins, as they ran, mounted their horses and rode away.

The situation at the stables was a true scuffle with many casualties on both sides when Enrique and Ruben showed up through the back entrance thus cutting off the raiders' escape; and they, to a man, yielded and threw down their weapons; this action not being accepted by Antonio's men who insisted on putting the raiders away for good. The Bragelone brothers finally managed to control the indians who found some solace and comfort in tying up their victims as tight as they could while at the same time directing to them mockery and some choice insults in their own language and in the Spanish they had learned form their overseers and other instructors. All the criminals were rounded up and held under guard, to be turned over to Captain Julio Montes and his soldiers on the next day, the wounded receiving first aid as a gesture of humanitarianism form Doctor Enrique Bragelone, for Doctor Mendez had fled from the scene.

.

JOSÉ VALDEZ

48

Don Felipe Finally Wakes Up and Makes Amends

During all that happened Don Felipe had not been aware of the spectacular events until one day when not totally under the influence of alcohol, Lucia came to his bed and helped him dress. Don Felipe questioned Lucia, "What is all the din and commotion I have been hearing off and on, at odd times, for the past two day, or so?" Lucia answered, "Are you sure you want to know, Don Felipe?" "Of course I want to know, is it so mysterious that you should ask me if I want to know?"

Lucia went on relating the high points of all that had taken place before, during and after the duels, including the result of the raid on Don Carlos' hacienda. Don Felipe asked,

"And are you telling me that my wife and her two brothers instigated this act and proceeded to carry out the raid on All Souls Day?"

Lucia knew that if Doña Manuela found out that she had told Don Felipe, she would be in a lot of trouble; but having had plenty of mistreatment from her, she threw caution to the wind and told Don Felipe all the information about the sad ending of the raid, including rumors that Doña Virginia had actually taken a very active role in routing the attacking brigands at the water gave by wielding a sword in a manner any man would have been proud to perform.

Don Felipe admitted, "I always knew there was something special about that lady. How I wish she had chosen me instead of Carlos. So, the Twins were run off again. That is nothing to what they are going to get from me if they don't leave this place." Lucia then asked, "What about your wife, Don Felipe?" "She has a choice, she can stay or go with them, because from now on I am going to make something of whatever life I have left."

Don Felipe for once in several days took a bath, shaved and put on clean clothes. As he started to go out the front door he was hailed by his wife who inquired where he was going, to which he answered with a certain air of mock courtesy, "I am going to see my cousin Carlos to tell him I did not have anything to do with the All Souls Day incursion you had a lot to do with master minding this criminal action."

Doña Manuela's caustic retort, "If you had not been in your usual stupor, you would have known that on account of that half-breed, Pepe and Don Carlos who mollycoddled him, my brothers suffered greatly, and all we tried to do

JOSÉ VALDEZ

on All Souls Day was to get even in some manner." Don Felipe replied, "So, look what taking the law into your hands brought you, nothing but shame to you and your brothers; and even Virginia now knows to what lengths you will go in your racist attitude toward Pepe who hasn't done anything to you, and what he did to your brother was done on the field of honor, and was well deserved." Doña Manuela's last words were, "Be careful, Felipe. Those words may come back to haunt you." On hearing this, which to him sounded like a threat, Don Felipe's voice became strangely sardonic and in a low pitch, as he remembered her, asked pointedly, "My dear wife, can it be that you are threatening me, your husband?" Doña Manuela did not answer but turned around and left the room as Don Felipe went out the door.

Don Felipe tied his horse to the hitching post, knocked on the door of the main entrance and was ushered in by Juana who happened to be passing by on her way to the kitchen. Don Felipe was announced by Juana and was asked to enter the private drawing room of the family where Don Carlos, Doña Virginia, Luis and Pepe were having after breakfast amenities.

At the beginning the atmosphere was not necessarily conducive to amicable greetings until Don Felipe explained the reason for his visit. The ice broke when Don Felipe begged Don Carlos to relate some of the more interesting and comical aspects of the fiasco. Don Carlos assented and started by the confusion created by the drunken terrible trio and their cohorts, who were met head on by Doña Virginia, Luis and Pepe; and how that portion of the raiding party was ended or culminated on the high note by Juana's frying pan.

At this, all had a good laugh, and Juana who had been asked by Don Carlos to stay in case Don Felipe wanted a repast, was abashed at having been the center of attention when her action was related that had caused great merriment. Don Carlos then told Don Felipe about his and the Bragelone brothers encounter; and how the two unknown horsemen did not utter a single word hoping to keep secret their identity, until one of them, Teodoro, who was recognized by his voice, started shouting imprecations at Doctor Mendesfor running away from the field of action.

49

Don Carlos Takes Precautions, And Doña Manuela Plans New Tactics

Don Carlos had one more comment, "I could kick myself for letting both of them escape, never realizing they could run so fast; but I expect to square accounts with them if they ever stop running." At this last remark Don Felipe added, "Carlos, there will be very little left if I find them first." The discussion continued with the Twins as the main subject, and there were many opinions as to the best way to counteract the Twins' next move, which everyone agreed was bound to come.

After many and quite varied opinions were proposed, Don Carlos, in summarizing the discussion addressed the group, "As the saying advises that in union there is strength, I suggest that while this vicious situation persists, that we take measures to combat it. These outlaws that are manipulated by Teodoro and his brother, Doroteo, have become bold and insolent because they think that they can get away with almost anything, and that is happening because Captain Julio Montes and his police have been lax in the performance of their duties because by the time they decide to act, the malefactors have already disappeared. So, let us unite, help each other and try to find out what the targets of these brigands are so that we may catch them, and dispose of them one by one."

Don Felipe had some advice to offer, "These people are very treacherous, and I would like to be allowed to join in this campaign since, in a way, I hold myself responsible for a situation that perhaps I should have foreseen and done something to curb it." Don Carlos told him, "You are welcome, Felipe, and that is good advice."

It was Doña Virginia's turn to speak and her advice was well received by everyone, "Let us not walk or ride alone at any time, but at lest in pairs, and always ready for action." My dear Virginia, in the last few days I have seen a part of you that I have not seen before, and it makes me very happy." Don Carlos figured the group had other things to do, and was about to terminate the meeting when Don Enrique spoke, "There is one that thing that I think merits looking into, and that is having somebody on the inside notify us of the Twins' activities; in other words to have a spy in their midst."

Don Ruben looked at his brother and said, "Enrique, how are we going to plant a spy so that we can obtain the information needed?" Don Enrique continued, "When I was tending to one of the wounded, for after all, it is my bounded duty as a doctor to tend to anybody, one of the raiders offered to talk to me in private because he said that it was very important. Puzzled and curious to find out what he had to say, I managed to move him out of earshot of his companions and he began by telling me his name, Daniel Pardo. He added that he was sorry that he had taken up this way of life and wanted to make amends. He said that he wanted to help us do away with the evil influence the Twins had with most of his companions. I then asked him how he expected to help, and he answered that by letting us know when and where the gang was going to strike next. I finally asked him to let us know what he expected in return for such services if and when his plan worked, to which his answer was that he would work in any kind of decent job that will help him find his way back to society and peace of mind."

Don Carlos did not have anything to say at that moment, so Don Enrique added, "This Daniel Pardo seemed to me to be quite sincere, and that is why I would like some opinions from all of you, including Don Felipe." When another short period of silence ensued, Doña Virginia's advice was accepted by all when she said, "Anybody, no matter who he or she is deserves a second chance." With that, the meeting was adjourned.

After the All Souls Day fiasco, the Twins made their way to Doña Manuela's private quarters to regroup and receive the usual dressing down from their sister and plan for the future. Doña Manuela, in a nutshell, told her brothers, "As one famous man once said, the die is cast. So now that everything is now in the open, let us do two things —get people we can depend on, and change our tactics." Teordoro spoke, "I can understand about getting the right kind of people but what about the change in tactics?" Doña Manuela replied, "We tried a master stroke and failed. So from now on, we will concentrate on a program of harassment, of attrition, of small incidents, and if anybody tries to interfere, it will be too bad for this time we will be ready. We will gain control of La Morada in this manner, and this is the only way to do it, in my opinion."

50

Doña Virginia's Advice To The Lovelorn

Doña Manuela had one last advice, "Since somehow they found out about our plans and surprised us instead of us surprising them, some of a mystery because we were the only ones who knew, perhaps as the saying goes 'the walls have ears,' we will have to meet at Teodoro's house or find another suitable place for we must make sure nobody knows where we will strike next." Doroteo entered the discussion, "As far as getting people we can depend on, I can vouch for some of our people that were turned over to Captain Montes. It seems that Captain Julio Montes, after some deliberation, accepted the story that the All Souls Day incident was merely a prank that unfortunately was misunderstood and caused some unhappy results. One of the men who was arrested, one Daniel Pardo, further helped his cause and that of his companions by assuring Captain Montes that they were sorry they had caused any trouble, and in the future would try to be model citizens; whereupon all were set free with a warning from the Captain."

Doña Manuela closed the session, "Let us all meet tomorrow at Teodoro's house around 8 pm, and everyone try to be surreptitious as possible on your way to the meeting, and you, Doroteo, bring your friends making sure that Daniel Pardo attends for I want to talk with him. Finally, all of you try to come up with some ideas because we must be ready to take advantage of the approaching festive season of Nativity, New Year and Epiphany."

It was not as if Don Carlos had not noticed the subtle, at times almost imperceptible change in the relationship between Luis and Pepe, for after all, he had fully accepted Pepe into his family and Pepe, gratefully accepted such singular offering, it was that whether he realized it or not, Pepe's sterling qualities could not but create a certain air of ascendancy and inspire confidence even to those who did not know him as well as the residents of the hacienda.

Don Carlos marveled at the ease in which Pepe seemed to fit into any situation. Pepe was ready to help anyone even though helping would entail handling dirty or heavy articles, notwithstanding admonitions from Don Carlos and Doña Virginia telling him that in his position as supervisor and member of the family he cold easily find someone to do such menial jobs.

Pepe's speech was soft and at times measured as if inwardly he was not sure of the import of an expression. He was not ashamed to ask in order to learn, and the looks of acceptance from his listeners made him feel an inner glow of satisfaction that spurred him to further excel in his desire to 'belong' through the methodical learning of the language of the Spaniard.

All of this was perceived by Luisa who ever since she was a little girl, had at times, looked to her playmate rather than to her parents for advice and comfort; and this feeling of tenderness and loyalty carried into puberty as a feeling or emotion that gradually enveloped her being to such an extent that made her start wondering that if all she wanted was talk to Pepe and be with him all the time to the exclusion of anybody else, except her parents, it had to be love.

At the same time the overwhelming desire to love and be loved showed her that along with that wonderful feeling came the pain that could only originate from a suspicion that hers was an unrequited love. As far as her mother was concerned, there was an understanding between mother and daughter when Luisa bared her soul to her mother, including an unbearable anxiety when Pepe went to do battle in the field of honor against someone who was presumed to give Pepe a lesson in swordsmanship, a very dangerous confrontation which could have had dire consequences for Pepe.

All in all, as her mother advised, someone has to break the ice and you could be the one to make the first move, she told Luisa. When she heard this, Luis asked, "Mamá, is that the way you acted with father?" Doña Virginia, after a slight pause, answered, "It was not exactly the same type of situation because I was lucky to have a number of suitors, one of which I was partial to, who was your father, so my decision was not an easy one. However, you may be sure that had the circumstances been different, I would not have hesitated to exercise bolder tactics, within the decorum expected of a lady, of course."

In your case try to understand the difference in social level that has existed between you two up to know. Pepe is a well-behaved gentleman, and even if your father has given him status as his possible heir, he did not mention any rules of conduct, so Pepe, in a manner of speaking, remains in limbo as far as demonstrations of usual familiar acts of hugging, embracing or just plain hand-shaking." Luis, after deep thought said, "Thank you, mother, I think I understand my and Pepe's situation, and I know now what to do."

51

Felipe, Jr. Wants To Avenge His Uncles

Shortly before the Nativity season that starts with a Novena on the 16th of December, at which time also school vacations begin and lasts well past the New Year, Pablo Perez happened to be walking along with his pal, Pito, Felipe Jr., and the conversation turned to the events that had recently taken place in which Pito's uncles, the Twins had become involved. Pable made some remarks that cut Pito to the quick, "I understand that your uncles suffered some reverses from a veteran of the Conquest and from a mestizo who some say is quite a swordsman." Pito's curt reply indicated his disgust, "I wish I had an opportunity to take care of the upstart mestizo or even Don Carlos."

After a moment of silence he gave his opinion of the incident, "There had to be something that swung the cards in their favor; perhaps the Twins had one too many; maybe they underestimated the situation, who knows what; but of one thing you may be sure and that is that there will be retribution, perhaps by me." An idea then struck Pito to try to get Pablo involved in his state of affairs, "By the way, would you care to join me when the opportunity comes for me to engage the great mestizo swordsman? I think you will find it interesting seeing as how Luis has been seen in the company of Pepe, and you do remember the tournament, don't you?"

Pablo thought for a minute and said, "It would really be interesting, so count me in, but with the condition that the expected encounter be solely because of your desire to avenge in part the humiliation your uncle Teodoro suffered; and I trust that whatever situation develops will be devoid of any improper conduct. Pito assured Pablo that the only reason he wanted to harass Pepe, and also Luis if the occasion demanded, was because he felt it was his duty to erase in part the smudge in the family name, which was caused by an indian who did not have sense enough to know his place.

Pablo did not add anymore to Pito's last remark, but when he looked at the end of the long main street, he spotted Luis and Pepe who were walking toward them, so he nudged Pito, and pointing to Luis and Pepe said, "Talking about the devil, no pun intended, but your long awaited confrontation is here, sooner than expected."

Luis and Pepe had also seen Pito and Pablo, and Pepe stopped suddenly and asked Luis if he did not mind avoiding Pito and Pablo, but Luis was adamant. He told Pepe that he

JOSÉ VALDEZ

would not stand for anybody calling him a coward even if he understood Pepe's reason for avoiding the meeting that had to do with the family ties between Luis and Pito.

Ever since the understanding that Pepe was to be considered a member of the family, Pepe more and more felt at ease wearing the new type of apparel befitting his new situation, and his athletic body resting comfortably on a pair of shiny boots posed a striking figure which caused admiration, especially from Luis.

It had taken some time before he decided to effectively walk into his new position as he had reasoned that not accepting this attribute would somehow cause dissatisfaction to everybody in his new family. In other words, Pepe thought simply that since he had been offered this role and he had accepted it, there was no question that everyone expected him to play the part.

While his mind was wrestling with this and other items that nudged his attention, Pito and Pablo came within speaking distance, these two having chosen to walk on the same side of the street as Pepe and Lluis. Pito, without any preamble, went straight to the grain and in a tone of derision told Luis, "Cousin, you haven't improved in your choice of companions, don't you remember that old adage "La mona, aunque se viste de seda, mona se queda?" (Translated literally – a monkey may dress in silk, but still remains a monkey.)

52

Wishing And Doing Are Two Different Things

The last remark that Pito made, obviously was meant to be disparaging to Pepe because it alluded to the different type of clothing Pepe had been wearing recently. The answer from Luis was not long in coming, "My dear Pito, I do not know and I am sure Pepe agrees with me that the adage you quoted is a most appropriate one and could very well apply to many people we know." Pito did not relent, "You, sir, do you always rely on your friends to come to your aid, or are you so thick-headed that you don't realize when an allusion is made?" Pepe's answer did not leave Pito much room for recovery from his original purpose, "Caballero, and I use this term with reservation, when Luis gave currency to your remark, he was actually doing you a favor for neither of us had an acceptable idea of your intent; and as far as I am concerned, all of us would do much better if we went about our business instead of wasting time bandying meaningless remarks."

Pito could not contain himself, "Since you prefer a more direct method, Mr. Pepe, I am calling you a sneaky half-breed whose luck has run out; and I will lower myself in order to teach you manners, sincerely doubting that you will enjoy the sharp edge of my sword." Without losing his composure or showing any anger in his voice, Pepe advised, "Such an invitation can not be received without a vote of thanks that my sword will give you in a couple of minutes, which is all the time I will need to take care of you, no swagger or affectation intended."

Pito, boiling mad took his sword out and lunged at Pepe who in a flash parried and ran his sword through the anterior section of Pito's upper right thigh which caused Pito to fall in a heap while Pepe put away his sword and Luis tended to his cousin until help arrived. On seeing his bosom friend friend falling from the wound inflicted by Pepe, Pablo could not contain himself and instinctively drew his sword, but at the same precise moment Luis jumped up and also drew his sword, while cautioning Pablo, "You have no quarrel with either of us, and I am sure that you realize it was a fair fight. However, if you persist, you will have to deal with me, and this time it will not be for sport." Pablo retreated and angrily told Luis, "I will yield for now because I understand reasoning, but I reserve the right to govern my conduct quite differently in the future." And with that, the field was cleared and Luis and Pepe proceeded on their original undertaking.

That morning Don Carlos had called Luis and Pepe and told them to ask the Bragelone brothers to come to the hacienda for the purpose of notarizing a document that he and Doña Virginia were ready to sign. When Enrique and Ruben arrived, Don Carlos asked if Juana and Pepe could be allowed to witness signatures, and Ruben disclosed that both of them would only witness Don Carlos and Doña Virginia's signatures, and not necessarily the content of the petition. All the time since his arrival from Spain and his ties of friendship with everybody in the family, there had been no allusion to the fact that Luis in reality was Luisa, so Don Ruben Bragelone was astounded that nobody had noticed any difference. So when he read Don Carlos' and Doña Virginia's deposition he wanted to be assured one more time that there had been a deception and that actually Luis was a girl. Looking all around the room including his brother, all he saw was that everyone knew something that he ignored up to that point. The affidavit having been executed, the Bragelone brothers decided to go to Mexico City, in person, Ruben, as the lawyer in charge of proceeding, and Enrique as the doctor who attended Doña Virginia during the birth in question, in case any other document was required such as a change of name from Luis to Luisa, in the annals of La Morada in general, and those of the family, in particular.

JOSÉ VALDEZ

53

Luis Is Now A Girl, But Has No Dress

The lengthy legal operation (also entailed a three of four day trip to Mexico City) had to be completed before word got around to Doña Manuela who, without a doubt, would find ways to stir up trouble. With this in consideration, the brothers wasted no time getting all the documents that had to be attached to Don Carlos' petition and started on their way to the Capital.

The business with the Bragelone brothers having been done, as far as they were concerned, Luis and Pepe decided to go for a walk to unwind from the excitement, in a very happy mood and somehow, surely not through Pepe's choice, the conversation veered around what conduct this was to follow after the changes concerning her became legal.

After the filing of the necessary documentation, which had to be after the return of the Bragelone brothers, Luis wondered, "Will I have to wear a dress like other ladies?" She said this in a joking manner, and she and Pepe had a great laugh. Along with this question Luis pointed out that she did not have a dress; in fact, she added she never had use for one. Pepe told her that she did not have to, but if need be, she could always borrow one form her mother, since she and Doña Virginia were about the same height and build.

When the conversation got around to how she would look in a dress, Pepe colored visibly and babbled something like Luis should continue in the same manner of attire. Luis agreed that for the moment that was the course to follow, but pointed out to Pepe that her question had remained unanswered. Pepe was fit to be tied because he did not know how to extricate himself from the course the conversation was following when Luis, with the utmost candor of a lady devoid of inhibition, tried to explain to Pepe that Mother Nature kept advising her to either get a bigger coat made or quit wearing one. "You understand what I mean, don't you, Pepe?" At this question he could only stammer, "I suppose so." Pepe did not even comprehend what he said or why he said it. While this conversation was going on, the pair arrived at the door of their home, just as Luis was preparing to add to his discomfiture by directing more leading queries and quips to Pepe, something in which ladies seem to have decided advantage, especially when young lovers engage in verbal sparring. Pepe gave a sign a relief when both crossed

JOSÉ VALDEZ

the doorway and reported all that had happened earlier, since there had been no time to do before. When he was told what had happened to Felipe, Jr., he decided to keep his counsel until word got around from Doña Manuela.

When Pablo and his friends arrived at Don Felipe's estancia, (the family preferred estancia to hacienda or rancho), Doña Manuela was not there, having gone to the Twins' home to explore the possibility of action in order to take advantage of all the activities in connection with the festivities which seemed to have earlier than usual, the accepted beginning, although not a fast rule being November 22nd, the fiesta of St. Cecilia, the patroness of music. When the messenger gave the news to Doña Manuela, she started her usual imprecations and asked for a lackey to get her carriage ready, all the time venting her anger in as colorful a language as one that a mule skinner could not improve upon, as she kept imagining the worst. When she arrived home, her husband, Pablo and Doctor Mendez were in the room where Pito was lying in bed. She rushed to her son while Doctor Mendez and Don Felipe assured that there was absolutely no danger, and Pito would be up in a couple of weeks.

54

Doña Manuela Files Charges Against Pepe

This did not console Doña Manuela until Pito told her to stop treating him like a child, and that he was all right. She turned to her husband and said, "What are you going to do about this, Felipe?" Don Felipe answered, "What the reason was for this fight is beside the point, but the fact remains that Pito wanted to test his mettle as a young caballero should, and he came second best. He is at the age when he wants to spread his wings and fight his own fights." Doña Manuela answered, "If you are just going to sit back and not do anything, I am certainly going to do something about this indian who is bent on doing harm to all members of my family, as witness my brother Teodoro and my son Felipe, Jr. who is not even eighteen years old."

Don Felipe with an air of finality addressed his wife and had his say before walking out of the room. He told her, "Until I am sure that neither of them went out of his way to look for trouble, I will consider these as two unhappy incidents which will add to their experience." Doña Manuela mumbled something under her breath and walked out of the house, on her way to look for Captain Montes to file charges against Pepe for she was sure that there had to be a law protecting minors from such people."

Captain Julio Montes was not in his office at the time, so Doña Manuela had to wait about forty-five minutes during which time her heels cooled off but her temper did not; and what made the situation worse was that she had been told by the man tending the office that Captain Montes was making his rounds when all along the good captain had been reaping the benefits of a siesta. When Doña Manuela was about to give up, Captain Montes hollered at Juanito, who was the soldier chosen to be in charge while he rested, "Has anybody come looking for me?" Juanito dutifully answered, "Yes, captain, here is a lady that has been waiting for about an hour, and she says that you better see her now."

Captain Montes entered and profusely extended his apology, "My dear Doña Manuela, if I had known sooner, I am sure we would have taken care of your business." The acrid, caustic tone of Doña Manuela's rejoinder caused Captain Montes to bite his lower lip, "My dear captain, if you would choose somebody with some common sense to take care of your office during your absence (derision in her voice), I would not have waited so long to file charges against an indian who almost killed my son, Pito." Captain Montes replied, "Doña Manuela, if I hear correctly, all you have to do is tell me who this inhuman person is so that if circumstances warrant, I will have him picked up, and if I can convince the highest court in the Capital to grant me authority, I will have him whipped within an inch of his life."

Doña Manuela told him, "I am referring to Pepe who, without a doubt, has used witchcraft to persuade Don Carlos to adopt him hoping in that manner to obtain a certain amount of immunity or leniency for his evil deeds." Captain Montes promised that as soon as he straightened his office he would go to Don Carlos' hacienda and with all things going as planned, he would have Pepe in custody. When he seemed to agree with Doña Manuela and listened attentively to her narration of the incident, it was only for the purpose of gaining time to figure out all the angles of this difficult situation, and it was all he could do to cover his confusion and disconcert which he realized was being caused by his rash promises to Doña Manuela, for a confrontation with Don Carlos had never been in his agenda.

55

Doña Manuela Loses Another Round

After Doña Manuela left Captain Montes, and the Captain started to get ready to go see Don Carlos in the pursuance of his unhappy and highly undesirable duty, he was accosted by Luis who happened to be in the vicinity, on her way to visit her "padrino" Don Enrique Bragelone. "Captain Montes, what did my aunt want?" "Don Luis, it was some complaint, really nothing of any importance. Well, I have to go on some official business," he told her. Luis kept pressing the issue, "Doña Manuela is never one to waste her time on something that you say is of no consequence, so I have an idea that it probably has to do with my father." Captain Montes, in one last desperate effort to extricate himself, said, "Don Luis, I regret that I do not have any more time to share with you, but I look forward to the pleasure your company some other time." Captain Montes galloped away, not having heard Luis say that meeting again with the Captain could be sooner than expected.

In less than an hour Captain Montes was knocking at the door of the front entrance of the home of Don Carlos. Juana ushered Captain Montes into the vestibule while Antonio took care of the Captain's horse. After Juana announced the captain's presence, Don Carlos appeared at the door and invited the Captain to come into his office, at the same time asking the reason for his visit and offering to be of help. Captain Montes thanked him for his courtesy and added, "Don Carlos, I regret that this visit is of an investigative nature preliminary to a formal complaint that is going to be filed by Doña Manuela against Pepe accusing of assault which caused serious injury. You understand, Don Carlos, that it is my duty to listen impartially to all citizens, and that is why I would like to enlist your help in clarifying this incident."

At that moment Luis knocked at the door of his father's office and Don Carlos asked who was knocking, and Luis answered, "It is I, father, if you are not to busy I would like to talk with you." Don Carlos said, "Come in, Luis." Luis walked in and expressed surprise at seeing the captain; well, father, I will come back later, when you are not busy." Don Carlos told Luis, "No, Luis, stay because I think this discussion has to do with you, too, and you were saying, captain?"

The captain could not hide his uneasiness but proceeded, "As I was saying, in her complaint Doña Manuela also points

JOSÉ VALDEZ

out that Pepe took advantage of a minor, which Felipe, Jr. is."
Don Carlos addressed Luis, "You were present, weren't you,
Luis, when this happened? Can you tell the captain and me
what you saw? You don't mind, captain, for Luis may be able
to shed some light on what happened, in which case you may
be able to govern your investigation and other actions in this
connection with the justice that this situation calls for."

Luis then, went on to explain what happened, "We, Pepe
and I , were walking in the opposite directions to Pito and
Pablo who were coming from the other end of the same street.
When we all were within speaking distance, Pito addressed me
disparaging my choice of company using an old adage about
a monkey wearing a silk dress and I replied that the simile
could well apply to several people that I knew. Pito then
turned to Pepe and called him a half-breed that was going
to be taught a lesson. Pepe thanked him for an invitation
that would only last a couple of minutes that was all the time
he could spare and need to take care of him. Immediately
and without warning Pito took out his weapon and lunged
at Pepe, who a split second later took out his word to defend
himself. The deft parrying by Pepe, which Pito probably
did not expect, left him wide open and Pepe, then, stabbed
Pito in the area of the upper right thigh which disabled Pito
and in my opinion, Pepe could have inflicted a more serious
wound."

After listening to Luis' account of the incident, Captain
Montes advised that before any decision could be made, Pito's
declaration had to be obtained for official record, but agreed
that if Pito made the first move, anybody would have had the

right to defend himself. With that Captain Montes left to talk to Pito at Doña Manuela's residence.

As it happened, Pito acknowledged that he had attacked first and as far as he was concerned he did not want to press a charge as there was no base or ground for any. Doña Manuela did not agree, naturally, and in one last attempt told Captain Montes that Pito was a minor, also because was short month and some days from his 21st birthday. Doña Manuela was forced to desist, and walked out in a huff directing her steps to Teodoro's house, while leaving Doctor Alberto Mendez and Lucia with Pito.

56

The Bragelone Brothers Return While
Doña Manuela Wonders About Pepe
And The Terrible Trio Is On The Mend

On the next day the Bragelone brothers returned from the Capital and notified Don Carlos that the petition concerning Luis had been accepted but would not be effective until a period of 30 days had elapsed, from the day of the filing of the petition, which had been three days before. In the meantime, two expert scribes had been assigned to work amending the vital statistics. Also, a hefty payment of 100 doubloons had to be deposited in the office of the Viceroy, part of that money to defray the work of the scribes, and the rest to be deposited in the Kings' monthly collections chest to be shipped to Spain together with other revenues. Don Enrique assured Don Carlos that he and his brother did not carry on their persons such a large amount otherwise they would have deposited it on the spot. Don Carlos understood and began to make arrangements to put that amount of money together.

Meanwhile, Luis put away her plans to celebrate her change of status until after the next 27 days. All the family, including Pepe, thanked the Brothers for their conscientious work, and at the urging of Doña Virginia, something Don Carlos had already planned with her, a document was drawn which conferred on Don Enrique and Don Ruben power-of-attorney on both of them, plus sizable dividends in the silver mining enterprise, which operation had been held in abeyance. The Bragelone brothers were apprised of all that Don Carlos and Doña Virginia offered them and they accepted; assuring the family of their loyalty and service in taking case of Luis' situation plus the appending of another name to Pepe on the baptismal certificate on file at the church, which certificate was to be considered legal for all civil transactions.

Ever since word got around that Don Carlos had legally adopted Pepe, Doña Manuela had been in a dither because she could not figure out a situation that she considered very strange and without any sense at all to her way of thinking. If Don Carlos wanted to do something for Pepe all he had to do was give him a more important job, or give him money, clothes, anything else but not adopt him, a half-breed at that. Again, Don Carlos did not have to adopt Pepe because it would be a sort of empty gesture because Pepe would not inherit anything for Luis, obviously, would not relinquish his statue as the family mayorazgo. It was plain to see that she did not yet know that Luis was a young lady.

JOSÉ VALDEZ

Was this a philanthropic action? And why? Was it because Pepe was Juana's son? Or trying to compensate Pepe for the loss of his father, who was killed protecting Don Carlos' property? She knew there had to be a reason but no matter how much she thought about it, she could not arrive at a plausible answer; and then she thought about Juana who could shed some light on the subject. If the problem was how to inveigle Juana, she figured that the only way to talk to Juana would be when she attended one of the many ceremonies during the holidays. One more thing that Doña Manuela did not realize was that the adoption of Pepe could very well, in the future, pose a threat to her original plans, if she was to take in consideration that the contract between the families was still in effect.

Notwithstanding the poor showing of Doctor Alberto Mendez at the Old Souls Day incident, and the dislike and hostility that the Twins displayed toward him, his services were still needed by Doña Manuela and the Twins, as witness to the fact that he was called to tend to Pito's wound. Since there were only two bona fide doctors in the community and it was obvious that Doctor Enrique Bragelone was not expected to be called either by her or her sons, Doctor Mendez continued to ply his trade among his regular patients and those of the friends of the Twins, some of which were Toton with a broken leg, Lardon, two broken ribs and Tamon who had been stabbed on his right leg by Doña Virginia. All things considered, Doctor Mendez had a flourishing practice, if he would only stay away from other activities. There was no denying that Doctor Mendez' ministrations had done wonders for the followers of the Twins, especially the terrible trio – Toton, Lardon, Tamon, but the infirmities suffered on the ill fated outing were of a nature that required plenty of rest, and this forced delay in their plans caused the Twins and Doña Manuela to be very unhappy, but her brothers tried to drown their disappointment in their favorite tavern, while Doña Manuela could only chafe and seethe at the enforced period of inactivity while looking for a chance to accost Juana on her way to church.

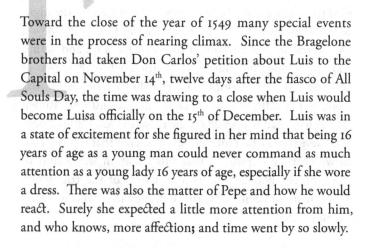

57

Lardon And Tamon Try To Jump The Gun – Pilgrims, Posadas And Piñatas

Toward the close of the year of 1549 many special events were in the process of nearing climax. Since the Bragelone brothers had taken Don Carlos' petition about Luis to the Capital on November 14th, twelve days after the fiasco of All Souls Day, the time was drawing to a close when Luis would become Luisa officially on the 15th of December. Luis was in a state of excitement for she figured in her mind that being 16 years of age as a young man could never command as much attention as a young lady 16 years of age, especially if she wore a dress. There was also the matter of Pepe and how he would react. Surely she expected a little more attention from him, and who knows, more affection; and time went by so slowly.

Doctor Mendez continued to perform miracles. Pito was up and about, although with a slight limp, at the end of three weeks, thanks to the resiliency of youth, Doctor Mendez' potions and the ministrations of Lucia who supplanted Doña Manuela while she was staying at the Twins' home, keeping house for them and helping with the care of the terrible trio. The trio, with the exception of Toton who was taking a little more time in his recovery on account of his broken leg, was doing fine. In fact, Lardon and Tamon had felt so well that their enterprising nature, without the knowledge of the Twns' drove them to try a couple of outings on their own but were thwarted by the untimely appearance of two horsemen; and if it had not been for the efficacy of the doctor's brews, they would not have found sufficient quickness to reach their horses and escaped with only a few minor scratches.

The reader may have guessed that the two horsemen were Don Enrique and Don Ruben who knew in advance of the planned capers of Lardon and Tamon form Daniel Pardo, who had been one of the assailants at the stables on the night of the 2nd of November. On that occasion Daniel Pardo told Don Enrique that he wanted to mend his ways and would start by giving the Bragelone brothers advance notice of planned criminal attempts. Obviously Pardo's scheme was working perfectly, and when Don Enrique and Don Ruben related what had happened on their visit to Don Carlos' home they were reproached for not having shared that information, to which they responded that this situation was a spur of the moment plan by the two members of the trio,which action had not been authorized either by the Twins or Doña Manuela.

JOSÉ VALDEZ

Seeing the hacienda, in its totality being saturated with the holiday spirit by the entire household, which operations were being supervised by Doña Virginia in the hallways leading to the ante chambers and bedrooms, by Juana in the sprawling kitchen and dining area, and Luisa, who was taking her new role seriously, in her father's private quarters and the two foyers, gave Don Carlos plenty to worry about because he was made aware of the fact that the days of much activity would soon arrive. It did not take very deep thought to arrive at the conclusion that everyday until the Epiphany (6ᵗʰ of January – Adoration by the Magi) robbing, stealing, mugging and other forms of lawlessness would be on the increase because the majority of people would be attending church rites. Based on a thinking that had become quite normal, Don Carlos decided to call a family meeting to decide a schedule of attendance at church liturgy and celebrations, plus the "posadas" which was strickly a traditional family celebration, a custom that had been an integral part of the Christmas Season for hundreds of years, during the nine days from the 16ᵗʰ of December to the 24ᵗʰ of December.

Basically the posadas is a folklore tradition which reenacts the tribulations of Joseph and Mary, who was with child. Tradition has it that Joseph and Mary, obeying the edict of Caesar, traveled to be included in the census being taken at the time. While seeking shelter, which was denied to them in various inns, in the town of Bethlehem, Joseph and Mary were forced to spend the night in a stall where our Lord Jesus was born in a manger on the night of the 24ᵗʰ of December. In accordance with the custom, families in a neighborhood get together and file from house to house asking for shelter while singing a traditional tune with the same traditional words. Naturally, when the group of pilgrims get to a house and ask for shelter, the people inside refuse for whatever reason, and the procession of pilgrims continues on to the next house, and the act is repeated again until in a predetermined house the pilgrims are invited to enter, and a great time of friendship and conviviality is enjoyed by all.

When the group of pilgrims is finally invited in, usually at the house of Don Carlos where there was room for all, the feasting and fellowship with accompanying jesting, joshing and pleasant bantering fueled by plenty of food and drink; but the main fun and laughter was derived by the breaking of the "piñata" by the children. The piñata is a big earthenware pot which is filled with all types of goodies, mostly candy, which fall when the pot is broken by one of the children who happens to hit it at the right moment, because the piñata is held by a piece of rope which being thrown over a cross bar allows one of the older posada participants to lower or raise the piñata in order to make the blindfolded child miss, whose turn it is to try to break it with a beautifully garlanded stick.

58

A Dress For A Young Man, Pepe
Goes To Finishing School

All these coming events kept disturbing Don Carlos, not for himself for in his life he had weathered may troubles, and even now seemed to be fraught with turbulence; but for Virginia, Luisa and Juana and the rest of the household who were also fair game for the predators which were followers of the Twins who would try to do harm to anyone connected with Don Carlos' hacienda, if for no other reason than to strike at him in that fashion. It was at times like this when submerged in uneasy thoughts that a ray of comfort would appear upon the realization that Pepe was his right arm, and he was not alone. Pepe was strong, fearless and resolute and his audacity spelled deep trouble for any troublemaker. Pepe was tireless and always ready for action, and Don Carlos knew that he could trust Pepe with the life of any person dear to him. It was laughable and absurd, but Don Carlos would sometimes entertain the idea that Martin had come back in the person of Pepe, to be at his side.

On the 14th of December several incidents of note occurred and before disclosing any, Don Carlos waited until the entire family gathered for the evening meal. Toward the end of the repast Doña Virginia asked her husband pointedly, "Carlos, are you going to wait until tomorrow?" That query, coming out of a clear blue sky, made Luisa and Pepe stop their conversation and look at Doña Virginia and Don Carlos. With a glint in his eye Don Carlos offered, "I was thinking to wait until tomorrow." "What is it, mother?" Luisa asked, "Does it have anything to do with us?" Pepe then inquired, "Is it something I have done?" Don Carlos waited no longer and said, "We were going to wait until tomorrow to spring on each of you a surprise." Luisa then asked, "While your father and I were in church talking to a prelate from the Capital, a Jesuit priest from Northern Spain by the name of Manuel Bermudez, who has been assigned temporarily to this parish to help Father Damian on account of the influx of parishioners during the festival season, a messenger arrived and delivered a package to Juana, addressed to somebody by the name of Luisa Monsibais de la Fosa." Luisa could not contain herself, "It's a dress, I know it's a dress, where is it?" Don Carlos told her, "Wait, Luis, there is plenty of time for that, and now I have to talk to Pepe." It was Pepe's turn, "I may not act like Luis, but inside I am just as anxious to hear what you have to tell me." Don Carlos took an air of seriousness and told

Pepe, " Don Marco di Georgio, who as everyone knows is the Master of Arms, wants you to come by his place to finish your course in swordsmanship so listen well to him and learn, for who knows, the knowledge he will impart may save your life and the life of others, too.

Pepe did not know what to say and mumbled a thank you in a quiet voice for he was overwhelmed. He was startled out of his reverie when Luisa tugged at his shirt and fairly dragged him to see the dresses he was to wear whenever the occasion demanded. For the present, however, she knew that she would wear and feel more comfortable with the apparel she had worn for so long. They went to look for Juana, who had made sure nothing would happen to the package by keeping it in the kitchen where she could keep her eye on it. It took but a few minutes for Juana to dress Luisa in her bedroom in one of the new gowns. When both came out and Juana had departed, Luisa came close to Pepe, who was astonished at what he was seeing that all he could say was, " Is that you, Luis?" "Yes, Pepe, do you like it?" she smiled. Pepe was flustered that he could only reply, "But you look so beautiful and delicate that if someone touches you, you will fall apart." It was then that Pepe realized what he had said, and he felt even worse when Luisa retorted, " Why don't you try to see if I fall apart?" Pepe sat down and had lost his power of speech when Luisa sat next to him and held his hand. His feeling defied explanation. When he was a child his mother embraced him and kissed him, and all those caresses made him feel happy, secure and loved. But this, this was different; he did not know how to cope with it; he did not know how to respond or what he was supposed to do, so, and his hands were actually shaking. Luisa was close to him and looking at him, and all he could do was lower his head and look at Luisa's beautiful hands.

Footsteps coming down the hall brought a welcome respite to his confusion, and he stood up and started examining the paintings on the wall while Luisa went to meet her mother who had shown her face on entering the antechamber. While the usual chit-chat was in progress between mother and daughter concerning all phases of the dress Luisa was wearing, Pepe saw an opening to make exit, and addressed them, "Pardon me, ladies, but according to instructions from Don Carlos, I am supposed to go to the Academy to see Don Marco di Georgio who wants to talk to me." When permission to leave was granted, Luisa, devoid of any reserve told Pepe as he was leaving, "Hurry back, Pepe, because you really haven't told me how you like this dress." Doña Virginia added, "Pepe, we will pray that everything turns out all right for you." With that, he thanked Doña Virginia, and left.

Don Marco di Georgio had closed the Academy for the holiday season, so he had plenty of time to devote to Pepe, who at that moment knocked at the door and was asked to enter. Don Marco started the conversation, "Good morning, Pepe," and Pepe answered "Good morning, Don Marco, although I was sent to you by Don Carlos, it was very nice of you to receive me." "Don Marco told him, "I guess you know the reason why you are here, and I add that it is a shame you could not have started your education in this field earlier, but I hope you can see that sometimes a society imposes certain rules whose failure to obey or conform to them can cause painful sanctions. But no matter, from what I understand

JOSÉ VALDEZ

you are quite a swordsman." Pepe had to clarify his position, "Thank you, Don Marco, and I understand your point of view and I trust that in time I will not try to judge anybody before I have all the facts." Don Marco responded, "Well put, Pepe, and since Don Carlos, who is my best friend has taken you into his family, I can do no less for you; so let us get started." The session lasted about an hour during which the Master of Arms demonstrated his repertoire of lunges, thrusts, passes and parries, some of which Pepe had not even dreamed about, but somehow, perhaps because of his great speed, and sheer strength managed to negate and answer with respectable execution. At the end Don Marcos told Pepe, "You are one of the strongest persons that ever handled a sword, and with a month's practice you will become one of the most talented and skillful swordsman I have ever come across in my life, and I am proud to be the one who will help mold you into a work of art, if I may use that expression." Pepe then said, "Don Marco, I will be forever in your debt, and I would like to impose on you for the practice that you mentioned; and now, with your permission, I will retire for Don Carlos has some things for me to do." "It was a pleasure, Pepe, and say hello to Don Carlos for me," Don Marcos needed. Pepe left quite happy at having crossed swords with a famous Master of Arms.

59

*Doña Manuela Weaves A Web, Daniel
Pardo's Fate Hangs In The Balance*

Lardon and Tamon held a discussion with Toton, who was almost ready to join the gang because his broken leg had already mended; and the theme of their conference was the mystery of the two caballeros who appeared out of nowhere to spoil their capers. The problem called for finding out if somebody within their organization had tipped off the night riders that Lardon and Tamon had encountered both times. Another aspect of the problem was whether the Twins and Doña Manuela should be notified. This part of the puzzle required much discussion, not whether the leaders should be told, but who was going to do the telling. Finally, it was decided that Toton would be the one since he had nothing to fear due to the fact that he did not go along when his brothers decided to jump the gun.

Oddly enough, when Toton told the Twins and Doña Manuela about is brothers' escapades, they did not seem overly concerned in the caballeros ill-timed appearance, but in why they were there. Lardon and Tamon were sent for and all three were questioned in order to find out who of the gang could have been close enough to the terrible trio to know when and where Lardon and Tamon were going to operate. After a spirited deliberation the trio agree that there were only two members of the organization present at the time – one, a fellow by the nickname of Bobito, which epithet is a diminutive of Bobo", a thick-witted, simple minded individual; and the other was Daniel Pardo, who had always been considered a member in good standing. Doña Manuela voted to eliminate Bobito because of his lack of brains to become an informer, to which Teodoro commented that Lardon and Tamon had not used much sense either by contravening the instructions of the upper echelon, which could jeopardize the plans for a big strike. Doña Manuela continued, "Let us find out if Daniel Pardo is the informer, and the only way is to make him fall into a trap. You, pointing to the trio, start planning another nightly visit to some pigeons' place, in a secretive manner tone but making sure that Daniel overhears. Give enough information to make sure of two things – that Daniel is the spy who will cause the cause the caballeros to appear again, and that Teodoro or Doroteo are hidden nearby to see what happens. The meeting closed and Doña Manuela felt quite smug at the plan she had devised, which was to be executed on the 16th, two days hence.

Around mid-morning of the 15th, Doña Virginia, Luisa and Pepe were carrying on a conversation on when and which church ceremonies to attend the next day in the evening, and without disturbing the process of the rites, when Don Carlos came in and announced that he had some news. First of all, he said, "As you all know, the ceremonies are classified as of a devotion nature, and only the midnight mass on the night of the 24th, and/or the masses of the 25th and New Years are designated as rites of obligation. Also, as regards this last precept, Fr. Manuel Bermudez has advised that special dispensation by the Bishop is to be granted on account of the difficult times that seem to be developing in this region as the climax of the season approaches. This dispensation applies to the persons that remain at home for protective purposes, so that means that other members of the family should attend services. By the way, Pepe, I saw Don Marco and what he told me makes us all very pleased; and what our new young lady, when is she making her debut?" Luisa answered, "I have been planning maybe tomorrow night, but I would not want to cause much commotion." Doña Virginia was about to say something when some rapping announced that someone was at the door. Doña Virginia called Juana, "Juana, will you please see who is at the door?" On opening it, she announced, "It's Don Enrique and Don Ruben."

"Come in, cousins," greeted Doña Virginia. What brings you here today, of all days?" Don Ruben spoke, "I told Enrique to wait until tonight, but he insisted that there were many things to do like paying our respects and congratulations to quite a number of people." It was Don Enrique's turn, "I am not going to favor anyone, Ruben, but

JOSÉ VALDEZ

I want to congratulate Don Carlos and Doña Virginia on the arrival of their new daughter; we congratulate Luisa on the superb role she has played all these years; and we congratulate Pepe on the great strides he has made, and ask him to remind us not to tangle with him with or without a waspon." All had a good laugh, and in unison acknowledged and Pepe said, "Thank you, Don Enrique and Don Ruben."

Don Carlos then asked, "How is your spy performing?" Don Enrique answered, "That is something else that we wanted to talk to you about and ask your advice." It seems that the self styled terrible trio finally realized that there had to be someone supplying the information to the caballeros who waylaid Lardon and Tamon on the nights they went out, for there were two persons present when these two made their plans. One was a somewhat simpleton which answers to the moniker of Bobito, and he has been ruled out for obvious reason, and the other was Daniel Pardo, our man. When the Twins and Doña Manuela learned about this from the trio, it was decided that Daniel Pardo had to be trapped." Don Ruben continued, "The trio made out like there was nothing untoward, and acting secretive, planned for a 9 pm, making sure that Daniel heard them; and depending on what happens tomorrow night, the sham raid will prove that Daniel is the spy." Don Enrique the advised that it was clear that he and his brother were not going to show up, but how to find out the result of Doña Manuela's stratagem was the question. A discussion ensued, and the bell for the noonday repast sounded.

60

Doña Manuela's Bait
Did Not Catch Anything

While the family was enjoying a nutritious and very palatable mean, Doña Virginia pointed out that it would be a shame to lose the information source, and Don Carlos' opinion was that Daniel Pardo's services would have come handy for information concerning a bit raid that was bound to come. Pepe suggested that he would be glad to be at the place where the raid was supposed to occur in order to find out what decision wsa to be made about Daniel since the two caballeros were not going to make an appearance. Don Carlos thought it was a good idea but explained that Antonio was better suited for that kind of maneuver since he had plenty of practice operating in the dark while he had been courting Luisa.

As was suggested by Don Carlos, Antonio was given precise instructions on what to do. He was to be at the trysting place in plenty of time to try to find out whether anyone else showed up. He was told that he was to go on foot because a horse would betray his presence.

As was instructed, Antonio arrived in plenty of time and his in the shadow of some trees and heavy thicket that sometimes serves as boundary between neighboring properties. He did not have to wait long for galloping was heard at around what he judged to be 9 pm. Two horsemen stopped close to where he was but in the dark he could not tell who they were until they started talking to each other after a good while. Doroteo spoke,. "Personally, I think we should have brought some of the other fellows, for if the riders put in an appearance as expected, we could overcome them by sheer force of numbers and find out once and for all who they are." Teodoro said, "Doroteo, keep quiet and let us get ready."

After another half hour, Doroteo talked to his brother again because he was getting tired of waiting and said, "They are not coming, Teodoro, and that means this trick didn't work." "I guess you are right, replied Teodoro, "I wonder what our sister will do next,." The Twins left at a slow gallop that made it easy for Antonio to follow them at a respectable distance. When they arrived, they found the rest of the gang and Doña Manuela enjoying the cool night breeze wile imbibing some strong refreshments. Doña Manuela took the Twins aside to a clearing and listened to the result of their mission, within an ear shot of Antonio, and in a low voice kept saying, "I don't understand it. If it is not Daniel, then who is betraying our moves? Tomorrow we will try to figure out what to do next."

Their report and mission having ended, the Twins rushed to join their comrades in their libations, as Antonio stealthily stole away to rejoin the festivities at the hacienda.

At approximately 10:30 pm, at Don Carlos' residence, the pilgrims asking for posada (shelter) were being invited to enter, and at about the same time Antonio arrived, and being spotted by Don Carlos, followed him to the kitchen for privacy. Doña Virginia, Pepe and Luisa in her beautiful dress also followed and Antonio related his own pilgrimage, after which the consensus was that for the moment Daniel Pardo had weathered the storm. Don Carlos then told Pepe and Luisa, "You two go and apprise Don Enrique and Don Ruben of the new developments early tomorrow morning; and now that we have received what I consider very good news, let us all enjoy the fiesta. Antonio, you did a good job that shall not go without reward. Let us go break the piñata." Don Carlos and Doña Virginia left the kitchen and were followed by Antonio and Luisa who was in the rear trying to force Pepe to take her by the arm.

There was absolutely no need for Doña Manuela to try to talk to Juana to extract from her any kind of information about the reason why Pepe had been adopted by Don Carlos; an enigma that had bothered her for a long time. The reason why became clear to her mind when a friend of hers on the morning of the 17th, came to tell her some astounding news that she had witnessed on the previous evening. She told Doña Manuela that Luisa had been seen attending a ceremony, and there were all kind of commentaries, from the ridiculous to the sublime, but on one thing everyone was in agreement, the person that everybody knew as Luis, is she were a young lady, she portrayed a most beautiful one. Don Manuela's friend was just beginning to gather momentum when she realized that she was not listening ans was staring at her with a blank look on her face, so fearing that her news had caused a bad effect, she cut short her recital and left.

61

Doña Manuela Swears
Vengeance Against Juana

Doña Manuela stood as if transfixed for the better part of an hour and inquiries from her brothers went unanswered. There was no room in her mind for anything but the shock of knowing that for many years she had been duped; her nephew turned out to be her niece. There had to be commentaries all over about her being deceived by her own in-laws. There was not doubt about it, she had been tricked and Don Carlos, his wife Doña Virginia, Doña Virginia's cousins, the Bragelone brothers, and even Juana all these years had probably laughed and made jokes about her. There was no excuse for what they had done. Doña Manuela could not see any motive except to make fun of her and her family. Through her mind raced many memories of instances when she had been close to Luis in the years of Luis' infancy and everything had seemed what it was purported to be. There was no reason at that time for her to suspect that Don Carlos and his wife would concoct such an outlandish deception.

It was then that she thought she would receive some understanding and sympathy from Don Felipe. She would make him see what is own cousin had done. Before she arrived at the Estancia, as Don Felipe preferred his place to be called, something hit her like a bolt of lightning. In all the years that she had visited Doña Virginia, and from the time Luis was born, and later, when he was toddling, and even when Luis started walking, she had never held him in her arms. And she wracked her brain looking for a reason, but she could not come up with any solution. She was almost home when things began to take shape and little instances started to fall into place, much as a difficult puzzle that imparts to its solver. But there was no joy for having found the answer, and Doña Manuela felt only fury; and although there were many who participated in the deception, there was one person who bore more responsibility than any other –Juana. Each and every time that she was close to Luis, Juana would whisk him away under any pretense. "So, it was you," she said aloud to herself, "You will pay for your insolence, indian half-breed, I will make sure of that."

Don Felipe was taking a siesta when Doña Manuela fairly burst and woke him up with the news of Luis' metamorphosis, but to her surprise, Don Felipe already had received the news from Lucia who herself had learned about Luisa from people friendly to Doña Manuela who at times would come by to inquire about Pito's condition.

"What are you going to do now, Felipe?" she asked him. Rubbing his eyes he answered, "What do you want me to do? Anybody is free to do what Carlos and Virginia did, and, personally, I think that was a trick that took some doing." Doña Manuela was flabbergasted at hearing something she did not expect. "You call it a trick, Felipe," she yelled, "Don't you realize that what you blithely dismiss as a trick in reality was a deception, a masquerade, a lie to dupe us, to make fun of us?" Don Felipe replied, "Is that what you think, Manuela? The whole world was satisfied in accepting Luis as a young man, and just because Luis puts on a dress, a big problem is supposed to arise and cause you great discomfort?" Doña Manuela had one last biting remark, "If you can not understand that what was done in the spirit of deception – our deception, then it is useless to make you see the reason behind this whole situation was subterfuge, for you seem to forget that according to the family contract Luis could not have taken his place as mayorazgo if something had happened to Don Carlos in the interim. "Now, the situation once more is stabilized with Pepe as the mayorzgo, but, who knows, history repeats itself," she finished with an air of foreboding. Don Felipe ended the conversation telling her, "Yes, Manuela, perhaps history may repeat itself, but let us be careful for the next time it could go the other way."

JOSÉ VALDEZ

62

Doña Manuela Outlines
Her Daring Plan

Doña Manuela was going to make good on her promise, and for that she had to have diversionary tactics, and time her operation to the most propitious moment. She was going to teach Juana a lesson that she would not forget for a long time. She had noticed that Don Carlos' family was alternating at attendance at the church ceremonies. Don Carlos and his wife would go to church while Pepe and Luisa stayed at home and vice-versa. Her plan therefore was to get to Juana when Don Carlos and Doña Virginia went to church leaving Pepe and Luisa at home. Then, use a couple of thugs to break into the house of Don Eugenio Cuellar, which residence was situated about 2 to 2 ½ miles on the north side of the settlement and about the same distance from Don Carlos' hacienda. While this took place, she would send somebody to the hacienda to get Pepe and Luisa out of the house by telling them what was happening at the Cuellar domicile, and that help was needed. This last bit of her scenario was the easiest part for there were plenty of kids playing on the street or looking for small jobs in order to earn a few pennies for spending on a tasty morsel of food or on sweets, school being out for the holiday season.

Doña Manuela's plan had merits because if all went according to her time-table, she would then, knock at the front door of the hacienda as soon as Pepe and Luisa left to lend assistance to the Cuellar household, which in the meantime was being beleaguered by her two henchmen. As soon as somebody opened the door of Don Carlos' residence, she would force her way in and deal with Juana.

Early on the afternoon of the 18th, it happened to be Don Carlos and Doña Virginia's turn to attend church services and this was working perfectly for Doña Manuela's plan. Don Carlos' stay in church would give her enough time to take care of her business with Juana, and not much more, since Don Carlos and Doña Virginia would have to return immediately to the hacienda as it was their turn, also to invite the pilgrims after the posada, and everything had to be in readiness – refreshments, food and piñata.

After she took her brothers into her confidence, she asked for two of the best members of the gang, two that could be relied upon to follow others and instructions to the letter as timing was very important for the success of the operation. Teodoro chose two that his experience told him would be

JOSÉ VALDEZ

ideal for the job. Doña Manuela looked them over and asked, "Teodoro, if I am going to deal with them, I would like to know their names." Teodoro replied, "Sorry, dear sister, but there are no names as everybody goes by a nickname or moniker, and there is a reason or this custom. If a name is bandied around, the police will look for an individual that answers to that name because that name is inscribed or listed on some kind of document – birth certificate, baptism, marriage, police record, etc., whereas looking for a nickname is not that easy, and that is what we use in our closed circles. Also, almost everyone has a nickname which nobody minds because it is part of the camaraderie that prevails in our group, not the public." Doña Manuela was chomping at the bit, "All right, who are they?" Teodoro, for an answer went to the door of the inner chamber where the members of the gang passed the time amusing themselves while waitng for an assignment, and called, "El Tecolote y El Lapiz, come quickly." Doña Manuela looked at the two characters and for her there was no question who was who, for 'Tecolote' (owl) looked the type on account of his nose, and with a little bit of imagination 'Lapiz (pencil) also looked the type on account of his small head and elongated stature. Doña Manuela took her two strange companions outside to give them instructions and left to find her place where she could watch Don Carlos and his wife leave the hacienda, while Tecolote and Lapiz started on their way to Don Eugenio Cuellar's residence.

When his sister, left, Teodoro kept thnking about the possibility that something could go wrong, so, on his own, he decided to send three more members of the gang to lurk around the hacienda in case Doña Manuela needed help.

With that in mind, he went again to the inner chamber, which also doubled as a sort of oasis to take care of the inmates' thirst, and called for 'Mono', 'Pulga' and 'Calvo' to get ready to hide in the environs of Don Carlos' hacienda in case Doña Manuela needed some kind of assistance, cautioning them not to let her know of their presence. The trio – Mono, Pulga and Calvo which characterized, respectfully, their nicknames as Monkey, for his second-story ability, Pulga for his diminutive size and Calvo for his obvious lack of hair, picked up their tools of the trade and started out but stopped when they heard some remarks made by some members of the gang.

JOSÉ VALDEZ

63

Doña Manuela Finds Juana and Wishes She Hadn't

When the task force comprised of Mono, Pulga and Calvo were about to walk out to start on their mission, they stopped suddenly when someone shouted, "Cuidado con la Morada," (Careful with the purplish one). Pulga looked at his companions and asked, "What are they talking about?" Neither Mono nor Calvo had an answer, so all three required and demanded to know the meaning of the warning. The fellow that had shouted the warning, who happened to be 'El Prieto' (the dark-complexioned one), answered with the air of one who knows, "Don't you realize that by going around Don Carlos' hacienda you are liable to meet with Pepe, who is one of the best swordsman around this parts; but worse of all, you might meet "La Morada' who was Don Marco's best pupil?" Pulga continued, "So, who is this 'La Morada' and where did she come form?" Another inmate took the floor and offered, "You three must be newcomers. We refer to a young man that used to be called Luis, and now has turned out to be a young lady, who sports a purplish birth-mark on the right side of her neck, so she is described in our customary way as La Morada; so be careful because she is the best swordsman or should I say swordslady, according to Don Marco, the Master of Arms who, himself is a fantastic swordsman. The trio left silently and with some apprehension.

At exactly 4 pm, Don Carlos and Doña Virginia left in their carriage, with Antonio doing the driving; and about the same time at the residence of Don Eugenio Cuellar the two villains, Tecolote and Lapiz started on their housebreaking job. Doña Manuela quickly found and sent a kid who was playing in the street to Don Carlos' hacienda with instructions to tell whoever answered that somebody was trying to break into Don Eugenios house. Doña Manuela had seen Don Carlos and his wife leave from a vantage point some two hundred yards south of the hacienda.

Although she did not know, her brothers had furtively sent three more members of the gang to lurk around the hacienda in case Doña Manuela ran into some kind of trouble. The three henchmen, Mono, Pulga and Calvol with misgiving on account of what they had learned about La Morada (Luisa), hid in a thick-wooded area some one hundred yards where they could see all that could happen outside Don Carlos' residence, and waited hoping nothing would happen to Doña

Manuela, but ready to help her or, if the situation dictated, to save their hides by strategic withdrawal.

As planned, the gamin sent by Doña Manuela advised Pepe, who answered the door, about the trouble at Don Eugenio's house, and left right away. Pepe apprised Luisa and both of them with some uneasiness about leaving their post, decided to go and offer assistance to be beleaguered Cuellar residence.

Doña Manuela immediately knocked on the door and when one of the maids opened the door, Doña Manuela asked about Juana and was told that she was in the kitchen getting the food ready for the pilgrims walking in the posada. The maid then tried to tell Doña Manuela that Don Carlos' orders were that nobody was to be let in the house during his absence; but Doña Manuela forced her way in, and the maid objected no further since she had no way of knowing her intentions toward Juana. The discussion was heard by Juana who wondered where Luisa and Pepe were. She started out of the kitchen at the time that Doña Manuela was going in, and she pushed Juana inside the kitchen.

Juana was taken by surprise and was not about to wonder how Doña Manuela had managed to invade her terrain for something told her that she was in for a difficult time. Regaining her composure, she asked the usual question, while maneuvering as unobtrusively as possible hoping to grab something to counteract the attack that she was sure was coming, "What are you doing her, Doña Manuela?" she asked. While answering, Doña Manuela started uncoiling her whip, "I am here to teach you a lesson, indian, so that you do not ever again make fun of me." Juana had not found anything on the counter to defend with, and thought of gaining time. "But Doña Manuela," she said, "Perhaps you have been misinformed because I assure you that I have never made fun of you." Doña Manuela was obviously savoring Juana's discomfort, "What about all the times you practically snatched Baby Luis away every time I wanted to hold him?" By this time she was within striking distance, and Juana tried one last disclaimer, "Luis was to grow up as a boy, and your intentions were not know, so I only did what I had to do, so you go ahead and do what you have to do."

The pride and stoicism of her race made Juana almost glad of this confrontation if only to prove that she was a stronger woman than this white Spaniard. Doña Manuela had already hit her a couple of times, and Juana, without a wince or a whimper tried to yank the whip by grabbing it from the end but the roughness of the whip's raw hide made her palms bleed. Next she was going to try getting close to Doña Manuela even though she had spotted a small poniard stuck in her belt.

There was not other way, she had to show her castigator that she might succumb but she was going to extract as high a price as she could. On the next time that Doña Manuela sent the whip whistling, Juana ran to her and for an instant the long whip enveloped both of them, and Juana took advantage of her nearness to start choking her, making the whip fall to the floor. Doña Manuela then tried to reach her poniard but Juana anticipated her move and grabbing her wrist caused to let go of the poniard and it fell to the floor, also. The situation now had developed into a one-to-one and Juana now knew the tide had turned.

64

Aftermath of Juana's Hand-to-Hand Fight

Fear and desperation were holding up Doña Manuela because she felt her strength was ebbing away against the stronger Juana. While wrestling on the floor where first one adversary and then the other seemed to gain the upper hand, in the back of her mind Doña Manuela thought about her niece, Luisa, and Pepe who would be returning soon form the Cuellar residence. This made her redouble her efforts but Juana would not let go. Both women were heaving, panting and gasping for air, their dresses in tatters and their hair in a disheveled condition.

In one last Herculean exertion, when on top of Juana, Doña Manuela shook herself loose and ran out of the kitchen, into the hallway and gained the front door at the moment that Luisa was getting ready to enter. Moments before, when Doña Manuela started out of the kitchen, Juana got up quickly and ran as fast as she could in pursuit of Doña Manuela, for she was not to be denied; she did not start the fracas but she was going to finish it. As the two antagonists raced past the vestibule and reached the front door, two things happened in unison, Juana caught up with Doña Manuela and began pummeling her, and Luisa came in only to be rudely pushed aside by the fleeing Doña Manuela who without a doubt had had enough blows form the irate Juana.

Luisa stopped Juana who wanted to continue her pursuit, and closed the door while asking Juana what had happened. Juana was still so mad and excited that she seemed somewhat incoherent. Luisa sat Juana on a chair and tried to calm her, when she heard shouting outside. Luisa left Juana for a moment to investigate what the shouting was about, and saw the trio of henchmen coming to the aid of Doña Manuela. About that time Pepe arrived, after having disposed of Tecolote and Lapiz who fled after being seriously wounded, and he saw Luisa at the door. He was about to dismount when she pointed toward the three malefactors and shouted, "Go, get them, Pepe. I'll be right behind you."

Louisa left Juana in charge of Maruca and ran out to help Pepe while he spurred his horse toward the three villains, one of which was trying to help Doña Manuela mount his horse, as Doña Manuela's horse could not be found on the spur of the moment. Luisa's horse also had wandered away, so she started running to help Pepe, who had already dismounted and engaged the trio of Mono, Pulga and Calvo, at a place which was about one hundred yards away.

When Pepe dismounted and had charged the trio, Mono and Pulga drew their weapons and engaged him, while hollering to Calvo to come and help dispose of their single enemy. Calvo, who as having plenty of trouble getting Doña Manuela on his horse because she was so spent that she could not muster any strength, let go of Doña Manuela who fell ignominiously to the ground where she lay helpless. Although Mono was bleeding from a gash on his left upper arm and Pulga from a wound on his side, all three started pressing more, all the time aiming at the spot where the horses were. Luisa arrived and took on Calvo who, on seeing Luisa's birthmark, shouted at his companions, "It's her, it's La Morada. Let us go and get Doña Manuela out of here." All three dropped their weapons as a sign of yielding and ran to their horses, with Calvo and Pulga riding double, for the last part of Calvo's suggestion concerning Doña Manuela was not necessary, because whatsoever, she jumped on Calvo's horse and rode closely followed by the others.

Luisa rode double with Pepe toward the hacienda and by then, one of the maids was applying some slave to the welts that Juana had on her back from the whipping administered by Doña Manuela. Juana recovered sufficiently to explain what had happened after she washed her face and fixed her hair as best as she could under the circumstances, when Luisa asked how Doña Manuela happened to get in, the maid explained that she answered the door after Luisa and Pepe left to assist Don Eugenio Cuellar, and Doña Manuela barged in and cold not be stopped. Pepe was about to ask his mother if she wanted to rest a little, when a knock at the door announced that Don Carlos and his wife had returned from church.

65

Don Carlos Takes Steps To Get Even With Doña Manuela And Pepe and Luisa Finally Fall In Love

When Pepe opened the door, Don Carlos and Doña Virginia entered and for a moment stood dumbfounded at the scene before their eyes. The vestibule was in an unusual disarray, and everyone was in a state of agitation and excitement. It seemed that all present were trying to talk at the same time, and since Juana was in the midst, it was obvious that something must have happened to her. Luisa was consoling Juana, Maruca, the maid who opened the door when Doña Manuela barged in, and two other maids were hovering solicitously around Juana, and Pepe was close to his mother in case there was something he could do for her. After the initial surprise at seeing such a bizarre scene, one that they

　　　　　　　　　　　　JOSÉ VALDEZ

never would have imagined, and one that they did not know anything about, Don Carlos and Doña Virginia approached Juana to learn what was going on.

The first person to speak was Doña Virginia who asked Juana, "Whatever happened to you, Juana, and what is that on your back?" Juana answered, "Doña Manuela came into the kitchen and caught me unaware." Don Carlos then asked, "How did she ever get in?" It was Maruca's turn to explain, "When someone knocked at the door, after Pepe and Luisa left, I opened the door and Doña Manuela barged in and went straight to the kitchen." Doña Virginia asked Luisa, "Why did you let her in and why didn't you stop her?" Luisa, in an embarrassed tone said, "We were not here, mother. Pepe and I went to help Don Eugenio's family that was being attacked by two villains, we were told by a kid who came to the door to tell us about it." Pepe wanted to share in whatever blame and said, "It was my fault, Don Carlos, I should have gone by myself." Luisa interrupted, "I insisted on going father."

Don Carlos had had enough explanations for he could see clearly the machination of Doña Manuela and said, "Nobody is to blame, and nobody can undo what has been done. The clever Doña Manuela has duped all of us. She waited until we left, sent a boy with the news about Don Eugenio, you two left to help, and she forced her way in." Doña Virginia asked the obvious question, "Why Juana?" Don Carlos was not sure, "Perhaps to show to what lengths she will go to revenge herself. Revenge for what, I do not know. but perhaps if Juana will tell us exactly all that was said; at any rate, we will be on our guard and we will respond in kind, for she will not get away with what she has done, and of that you can be sure.

After looking at the welts that were still bleeding, Doña Virginia told Luisa to bring Don Enrique to treat Juana's cuts, bruises and welts. Luisa turned to Pepe and asked him to go with her, and Don Carlos added, "While you two are there, also bring Don Ruben who, as a lawyer, should be able to give us some advice on what course to follow as redress for Doña Manuela's acts." Luisa and Pepe left to find the Bragelone brothers as Don Carlos had requested. On their way, Luisa noticed that Pepe's left arm was bleeding from a gash suffered while attacking the three brigands who were helping Doña Manuela escape. Pepe had tried to control the bleeding with his handkerchief but caught in the torrent of activity of his mother's unprovoked attack, he had forgotten about his own problem, minimal as he judged it to be. Luisa reined her horse and insisted that Pepe do the same. She took out her own handkerchief and cleaned the wound as best as she could and dressed it with her scarf, all the while talking to Pepe in an endearing manner. It was pure ecstasy for both of them to be so close to each other and nature was not to be denied, for somehow, and neither knew how it happened, they embraced each other for the first time and sealed their long awaited promise with a chaste kiss.

After dressing Pepe's wound, they hurried to Don Enrique's house to have the gash examined and treated by the doctor. Both Luisa and Pepe were in reverie, and to be expected upon their recent expression of mutual love, daydreaming as to when they could be alone again, if only for a few minutes, to taste again the nectar of the gods.

Don Ruben was visiting his brother and after listening to Pepe and Luisa about the situation, all four rode together to

Don Carlos' hacienda after Don Enrique treated Pepe's left arm and made sure there was no danger of infection. When they arrived, they were told what Doña Manuela had done to Juana, and how through trickery she had managed to invade the premises to get to Juana. While Doctor Enrique was busy taking care of Juana, Don Carlos asked Don Ruben what action could be taken according to the law against Doña Manuela, and Don Ruben answered, "Don Carlos, since there is no court in this locality, and for that matter, no authority with jurisdiction over a Spaniard, and much less over a member of the aristocracy the only recourse is to file a suit against her in the High Court in the Capital. For the moment, however, and for the record, we should file charges with Captain Montes." Don Carlos assented, "Ruben, let us do that immediately." Don Enrique dressed Juana's welts and abrasions with ointment and prescribed as much rest as Juana could stand, and not too much exertion in order to give her system a chance to heal quickly. All this did not set too well with Juana who did not want to defer some of her duties to Maruca, who at odd times sometimes helped in the kitchen. Before leaving, the Bragelone brothers advised Don Carlos to save the whip and the poniard as evidence for future litigation.

66

The Two Felipes Learn About Doña Manuela's Reprehensible Conduct

Since the day was almost spent and the posada would be beginning in an hour or so, Don Carlos, his wife, Juana and the Bragelone brothers postponed their visit to the office of Captain Julio Montes until the next day, the 19th of December. On this evening, as luck would have it, Don Felipe and his son, Felipe, Jr., knocked at the door of Don Carlos' hacienda and were ushered into a large ante-room by Maruca, where Don Carlos, Doña Virginia, several maids and other servants were making preparations for the reception following the posada. There were tables with all sorts of viands, breads and meats; other tables with fruits, candies and related delicacies; and other tables where the plates, cups and glasses were set up well in front, so that the pilgrims could pick up whatever they needed for whatever they chose to eat or drink, or both.

Don Carlos went to Don Felipe and embraced him, and shook Pito's hand, while telling them how glad he was that they had decided to come to the posada. Doña Virginia, always the perfect host, greeted them effusively and bid them to take a seat, but Don Carlos decided tht this was as good as any to apprise his first cousin of what had happened to Juana; so, he told his wife to accompany Don Felipe and his son into his private office as he had something important to communicate to them. Don Carlos advised that he would be right in as soon as he gave the group in the ante-room instructions.

The two Felipes and Doña Virginia had not been in the private office more than two or three minutes, during which, naturally, some apprehension pervaded the atmosphere, when Don Carlos walked in, and in a non-committal manner asked everyone to sit, and directed his words to his cousin, "Felipe, I am asking you to believe that I regret to the bottom of my heart what we are going to reveal to you, and to Pito who is almost of age, and therefore, free to make up his own mind to conform to the situation as it now stands." Don Felipe, with a frown on his face spoke, "Carlos, you are talking as if something has happened that has to do with us, and I , myself am at a loss as to what we may have done, inadvertently." Don Carlos promptly pointed out, "Felipe, and you too, Pito, there is nothing any of you have done, but when and how a person related to you has committed an infraction which can not be condoned; and I am asking Virginia to relate to you in minute detail what happened this afternoon."

Using all names and as much detail as possible in order to place Doña Manuela's actions as objectively as she could, inasmuch as she was not present when the confrontation took place, Doña Virginia ended by advising her listeners that the objects that Doña Manuela used on Juana had been retrieved for legal action. She added that as far as more proof, Juana was suffering from the welts inflicted by the whip used on her. It was at this point that Pito, raising his voice denied that his mother would have been capable of such acts and called on his father to join him in demanding more proof of culpability. Don Felipe told his son, "I know how you feel, Pito, and it seems incredible that anybody would perpetrate such impropriety, but knowing her much better than you, and with the whip and poniard bearing her initials, I don't think that you as a Spaniard gentleman, would insist on the ultimate proof, which would be to force a woman, no matter who she is or what her station in life may be, to show you the result of the flogging."

Pito's spirit seemed to be crushed, and he looked so stunned as he kept repeating in a low voice, "Gran Dios," (Good God) "How I wish I had not come." Don Felipe tried to console him, "Felipe, it is said that ignorance is bliss, but believe me, it does not work forever, and eventually we would have learned the truth, and perhaps under more difficult circumstances." For a minute or two complete silence ensured in Don Carlos' office, when an insistent knocking not only broke the silence not only broke the silence but also stirred everyone into some movement after being motionless as a feeling of empathy for Felipe and his son, Felipe Jr.

Don Carlos having bid whoever knocked to enter, Luisa and Pepe entered the office. Luisa was the first to speak.

"How are you, 'tío', and you, primo (cousin)? Don Felipe, ever romantic, "I am fine, Luisa, now that I see that you turned out to be a beautiful young woman, don't you think so, Pito?" Pepe, in the meantime had approached Felipe Jr. and extending his hand told him that he held no rancor at all for anybody. And Pito shook his hand, and in a special look that was understood by both, thanked him for not mentioning anything else. After this action of friendship, Felipe Jr. took everyone by surprise by taking Pepe by the arm and both made their way to where Juana stood and said, "How are you, tía Juana (aunt)?" Pito's noble gesture held all spellbound, and Juana could not hold back her tears, "Felipito, I am so glad to see you." Juana was very emotional because she remembered that there was a great love in the past between her and Pito, when she used to have him hanging from her apron begging for sweets or cake that she would never deny him. Juana, between sobs, answered, "I am all right, Felipito, and I am so glad to see you." The scene touched everyone's heart and all had a difficult time staying dry-eyed.

Don Carlos broke the spell when he asked Don Felipe if he did not think that maybe all should have a drink or something to eat, and Don Felipe agreed and with Doña Virginia in their middle they made their way to the ante-room, followed by Pito and Pepe, and by Luisa and Juana.

At this time the pilgrims entered having been granted posada by Maruca and the rest of the maids who sang the welcoming verse. In the confusion, hustle and bustle, singing, talking and maneuvering around the tables, nobody paid attention to Don Carlos, Doña Virginia and the two Felipes who as much as they tried to join in the spirit of the celebration, their demeanor belied their feelings. Juana, in a light-hearted mood, as if a great weight had been removed from her back, made her way to the kitchen where she always reigned supreme. Luisa and Pepe found a nook, far removed from the noise of the gathering, and enjoyed each other's company and the food and delicacies their larceny had provided at great risk.

67

Charges And Counter Charges

Earlier, when Pepe and Luisa had run off the three henchmen and Doña Manuela had managed to mount Calvo's horse quite easily, she rode straight to the Twins' residence where Teodoro and Doroteo were astonished to see their sister in such disarray, and Mono, Pulga and Calvo, without their weapons and in a very disastrous condition. They wanted to know what had happened but Doña Manuela would not satisfy their curiosity except to tell them that she was in a hurry to file charges against Juana for unprovoked assault by an indian on a lady of Spanish Aristocracy. Doña Manuela wanted to appear in a state of dishabille to give more credence to her accusation; and to that purpose she changed only her upper bodice because in her struggle with Juana, the one she had worn suffered enough damage to make her feel quite uncomfortable when she tried to gather tatters of her upper dress to cover some delicate parts of her anatomy.

Doña Manuela was right in her thinking on two counts – by being there first with her accusation which provided a small and only temporary advantage, and by having Captain Montes predisposed to believe her story seeing her appalling aspect which gave the impression that she had just escaped from her assailant. After various questions by Captain Montes and slanted answers by Doña Manuela, Captain Montes touched on a ticklish subject, "If you will forgive me, Doña Manuela, what was the purpose of your visit, and why did you not wait until Don Carlos and his wife were at home?" "Captain Montes," she answered, "In the first place, I did not know that Don Carlos and his wife were not at home; and even if they had been at home, my visit was with Juana to congratulate her on her son, Pepe, having been designated as mayorazgo. Then, when I pointed out that it was a good stroke of luck they had made, and the changes and benefits they had obtained, she lashed on to me, and no telling what could have happened to me if I had not mounted sufficient strength to escape from the irate indian, and that is why I am here asking for justice." Captain Montes closed the meeting, "Doña Manuela, everything has been duly recorded, and I assure you that the law will take its course."

On the morning of the 20th, Don Ruben, as the lawyer of record, and Don Enrique, as the doctor in attendance of

Juana, entered Captain Montes' office and announced that they were representing their clients Don Carlos and his wife accusing Doña Manuela of housebreaking, and Juana claiming an unprovoked attack. Both charges named Doña Manuela as the perpetrator and the Captain was asked to take due note of the accusations. The Captain pointed out that Doña Manuela had filed a similar charge against Juana, which predated Juana's charge against Doña Manuela.

"Before going any farther, dear Captain," Don Ruben said with a little sarcasm in his voice, "Let me warn you that if you contemplate any kind of action against one of my clients, something like bail, surety, or any type of process, to get it out of your mind, unless Doña Manuela is subjected ot the same treatment." Captain Montes thought that Don Ruben had inadvertently given him room for a clinching argument, "But Don Ruben, Juana does not have any rights per se because she is a unit in the encomienda allocated to Don Carlos." Don Ruben was waiting for this captious argument, "By the same token, and following the statutes covering encomienda supervision, any indian member of the encomienda, to all intents and purposes, is the property of the administrator, and Doña Manuela has caused great damage to Don Carlos' property, to which my brother, Don Enrique, in his capacity as a doctor will attest." Don Enrique had had enough of the discussion and added, "Juana received great punishment form the whip used by Doña Manuela, and as her doctor, I can attest to the wounds received by this person who, in my opinion, is not a unit. As a doctor, I was glad to treat her wounds not only because she is a fine person, but also because of my oath that I am supposed to treat anybody and to try to save lives, although I feel at times like taking some that do not desserve to live." Without any more discussion Captain Montes closed the preliminaries in this case, for formal litigation was to proceed in the Capital.

68

Pito Sees Life From A Different Angle

After the posada, both Felipes rode back to the Estancia in silence, each immersed in his own thoughts and on dismounting, saw light in the living room which meant either Doña Manuela had returned or the house was being visited by some of the gang controlled by the Twins. Both dismounted with their weapons ready for action, and on entering, saw Doña Manuela who had just finished cleaning up and putting on a clean dress.

Doña Manuela spoke first, "I suppose you have come from the enemy's camp." Don Felipe answered, "Manuela, you know very well we have never been enemies. We have had our differences and some misunderstandings, but that is all." Doña Manuela had just begun her tirade, "And not only do you go humiliating yourself, but you have to take our innocent son with you." Felipe Jr. thought it was time for him to say something to make his mother know how he felt, "Mother, we are always well received at Don Carlos' hacienda, which is as it should be for we are all related; and even Pepe declared to me that he held no rancor because of the cruel treatment Tía Juana received from you." Doña Manuela's fury was on the increase, "Pito, to think that you have been consorting with idians is too much, and Juana is not your 'tía' but an Indians, and a crafty one at that, and Pepe is an upstart, a parvenu who, somehow, has wormed his way into Don Carlos' confidence, but neither Pepe nor his mother, Juana, are in our class."

Don Felipe was fast losing his patience, "Manuela, when are you going to get it through your head that all of us have been created by the same God, and that, therefore, we should try to get along with each other the best way that we can? I think I will look for Carlos' idea which is to grant his encomienda community certain privileges which in time will teach them to lead their own lives in our changing world." "Felipe," Doña Manuela added, "Your outlook concerning the encomienda and your ideas, in general, are just too much. I grant you that the same God created all of us, but this same God also created burros and other types of animals which are as far advanced as the ones I am talking about." Pito closed his end of the heated discussion by telling his mother that he regretted to learn that she had harbored such antagonism for so long.

Pito went to his bedroom, his mind in turmoil. He started seeing things that he had not been aware of before. His memory went back many years when the two families used to visit each other; and when earlier in the day his father invited him to the posada at Don Carlos' hacienda, he went along to please him and to have some company, for his mother had distanced herself from the Estancia, preferring to be with the Twins. Pito had entered Don Carlos' house with an air of reserve and aloofness as if he were being forced into a social function which, if he did not despise, the least he could say was that he felt a dislike for the behavior and conduct of all people, the goings on at all levels, the posadas and all the cheerful greetings, all of which he considered pretentious and artificial.

Expecting what he had in mind, Pito was amazed at the manner in which he was greeted and for a while he did not know how to comport himself. The familiarity permeating all around awakened in his long-forgotten feeling of friendliness and affection, and he felt drawn into the spirit of amity being displayed by all, including his father, that he had to admit to himself that it had been a long time since he had experienced such a wonderful feeling. This ambience also evoked in him memories when as a child he had unwittingly avoided the odious climate being caused by friction between his father and mother, his mother and her brothers and his father and the Twins; and he had made his way to his uncle and Doña Virginia, and found solace, comfort and love from everybody, and his every wish had been satisfied by Juana.

He also enjoyed the warm feeling of remembering the fun he used to have playing hours with Luis, and both of them going into the woods learning about animals, plants and other things of the wild under the guidance of Pepe who was always taking care of them. Pito reminisced about his early life and wondered why he now realized that it was son easy to make people happy, and how he had all these years been doing the opposite. He had neglected to attend church for a long time and a strong thought and desire came to his mind that maybe in the peaceful and serene mood of the church he could best examine his life and praying to God would help him find the way to redirect his purpose in life.

On the 21st day of December, early in the morning, Doña Manuela left the Estancia and directed her steps to the Twins' residence and Pito left soon after to look for Father Manuel Bermudez, while Don Felipe, after having a light repast prepared by Lucia, went to take a look around the Estancia with the express purpose of finding ways to improve his relationship with the indians in his encomienda, and also to try to improve the general conditions of life of his charges.

69

Don Felipe Persuades Don Carlos
Into Alleviating A Thorny Situation

From the time the two Felipes attended the posada at Don Carlos' hacienda and found out what Doña Manuela had done, to the morning of the 21st of December when Felipe Jr. decided to visit Father Manuel Bermudez seeking advice, Don Felipe and his son, each in his own way, reflected on what had happened not only in Don Carlos' residence but also in their acrimonious conversation with Doña Manuela, and pondered about the possible consequences.

They were apprehensive, naturally, and ready to welcome any solution, but at the same time they were worried of what the solution might be, for after all, it was the future of Don Felipe's wife and Pito's mother. With this in mind, Don

Felipe went to see Don Carlos hoping to convince him to use his influence in ameliorating the difficult situation, while Pito was on his way to talk with Father Bermudez, who at this time was quite busy hearing confession of the parishioners who wanted to avoid the rush later.

Don Felipe knocked at the door of his cousin's house and was ushered to Don Carlos' private office. After the usual amenities, Don Felipe stated the object of his visit which was to ask Don Carlos to use his influence in softening the impact that Doña Manuela's actions had created. Don Felipe pointed out that it was in the benefit to all members of the two families because of the scandal that was sure to follow. Don Carlos listened attentively to Don Felipe's loquacious argument but advised his cousin that it was a little bit late to try to change the course of the situation because Doña Manuela had already filed charges against Juana along the same line, and he doubted that Doña Manuela would cooperate in canceling her suit. Don Carlos also added that she had filed charges first, but if she retired her accusation, he would have Don Ruben do the same. Knowing his wife and how obdurate and unyielding she could be, Don Felipe felt disconsolate and left.

In the meantime, Felipe Jr. had an interview with Father Bermudez and revealed all that had happened and how his mother had acted, and asked the Jesuit priest for advice. The priest told him that he should, under any circumstances, forgive his mother, and pray that she change her way of thinking. As far as Pito's mentioning that he felt like embracing a religious life, the priest told him not to act too hastily, and to let the Lord decide the issue, and he could help

JOSÉ VALDEZ

his own cause by fervent prayer and attendance to church. Pito promised to take into consideration the priest's advice and went back to the Estancia.

When Don Felipe returned to the Estancia, he called his son to tell him about his conversation with Don Carlos. Don Felipe explained to him that Doña Manuela had filed suit against Juana charging unprovoked physical attack. He also added that Don Carlos was reasonable enough to agree to cancel his own suit against Doña Manuela if she were to agree to cancel her own suit against Juana. Don Felipe told him, "Pito, there is no other way to avoid scandal and bad publicity but to have your mother agree to cooperate; otherwise, she will be found guilty. You are the only one she will listen to, so I ask you to go to her and try to make her understand that it will be for the well-being of every member of the two families. Pito agreed and rode toward the Twins' residence.

While this was going on, Don Carlos called Pepe and Luisa and told them to go to the Bragelone brothers and ask them to come to the hacienda at their convenience, because of some very important developments. As luck would have it, Pepe and Luisa arrived just in time to prevent Don Enrique and Don Ruben from starting on their journey to Mexico City to file the documents outlining the accusation against Doña Manuela, so all four rode back to the hacienda to comply with Don Carlos' request.

70

Doña Manuela Hatches Another Plot
- Felipe Jr. Joins A Monastic Order

When Don Enrique, Don Ruben, Luisa and Pepe arrived, Don Carlos and Doña Virginia were finishing their instructions to the maids and other help about the preparations to receive the pilgrims comprising the group which is the traditional manner would sing the song requesting posada at a number of houses, where they would be denied lodging, before arriving at Don Carlos' house where they would be invited in. The vanguard of the group had started toward the first house, with four sturdy pilgrims carrying a square board on which the statues of St. Joseph and the Virgin Mary were solidly positioned. After that followed the group comprising the pilgrimage, and Don Carlos calculated that for about an hour or an hour and a half, he would have no interruption so he bid his wife and the four riders into his office.

Don Carlos spoke first, "Don Felipe came to us and requested that we try to lessen in some way this difficult situation, and we agreed providing that Doña Manuela cancels her accusation against Juana." Don Enrique then mentioned that it was providential that Pepe and Luisa showed up when they did because he and Don Ruben had already made preparations to go to the Capital to file the documentation for indictment procedures. Another stroke of luck was also mentioned by Don Ruben who told him that when they were ready to ride back with Pepe and Luisa to comply with Don Carlos' request, Daniel Pardo arrived with some important news.

I will be recalled that this Daniel Pardo was a member of the Twins' gang who after the fiasco of All Souls Day had been spying and revealing information about the gang's actions, and especially about the time when Doña Manuela sent Teodoro and Doroteo to find out who the unknown horsemen were who had been making an appearance at just the right time to thwart the gang's nightly forays. Don Ruben continued relating that Pardo had learned that Doña Manauela and the Twins had been following closely the movements of the Bragelone brothers, and planned to waylay them at the 'Venta de San Juan' (St. John's Inn), which is a sort of stopping place between the settlement and Mexico City. Pardo also added that rumors were flying that the Twins wanted to dispose of him because he was suspected of being responsible for anything that had been going wrong. For that reason he was afraid for his life if he went back to the gang.

Don Carlos explained to the Bragelone brothers all that had transpired in his latest conversation with Don Felipe, and also advised that if Doña Manuela remained unyielding, then they should take Pardo and Antonio with them on their trip to the Capital, and Pepe and Luisa would also accompany them as far as the Venta de San Juan, and these last two would then return to the hacienda to be ready to deal with any untoward activities of the gang members remaining at La Morada.

On the 22nd of December Don Felipe told Don Carlos that Doña Manuela had flatly refused to cancel her charges against Juana despite the entreaties of her son; and that caused Felipe Jr. to become quite despondent and would not talk to anyone. That, naturally worried Don Felipe who imagined all sort of dire actions by his son; but when Felipe Jr. finally talked to his father, it was to tell him that he had decided to embrace a religious life, and to that effect he was going to see Father Bermudez to obtain a litter of introduction to the General of the Order of the Society of Jesus. He resigned himself to practically losing his son although in a way he was glad that his son was not going to be under the evil influence of his mother anymore.

On the other hand, since Felipe Jr. was to become a monk thereby renouncing all worldly goods, the family of Don Felipe would be left without a mayorazgo, and no telling what Doña Manuela would do when she would find out that Pito had decided to join a monastic order.

JOSÉ VALDEZ

71

Confrontation In the Offing At St. John's Inn

After the last two disasters, the breaking into the Cuellar residence which was a diversionary tactic, and Doña Manuela's ignominious escape from Don Carlos' hacienda where she received a generous pummeling from Juana which treatment discolored the skin on her back, the Twins and their sister remained unusually quiet and peaceful. The reason for their uncommon behavior was two-fold – to have the members who had been in action recover from their wounds, and plan how to stop the filing of the documentation accusing Doña Manuela which might seriously curtail Doña Manuela's freedom of action if she were to be found guilty, which seemed to be a very likely outcome. Another worry that was fast becoming annoying and most inconvenient was the fact that being idle, and with no extra income to take care of the well known habits of the gang, Doña Manuela was spending quite a bit of her own income, which being ample for herself, was not sufficient to keep the entire company in a happy mood.

While this was taking place, and giving credit where credit was due, Captain Julio Montes had not been inactive all this time. Knowing the principals and the delicate situation that Doña Manuela created, he could visualize that his position was precarious and he could lose his post if he made the wrong move. On one side he could see the Twins and their cohorts, and he admitted to himself that in a pitched confrontation he could not rely too much on his underlings who were in too thick with the Twins from whom they received from time to time generous stipends that augmented their meager pay. On the other hand, he could see Don Carlos, a paladin in the Conquest of New Spain and a close friend of the Viceroy, Don Hernan Cortés. Ever since Doña Manuela had committed her infraction, Captain Montes had wrestled with his conscience putting his future on the same scale as the pursuit of justice. It was a very difficult decision he would say to himself, almost a no-win position, having spent some sleepless nights during which he studied at length all the facets of his predicament, the scale tilted in favor of justice when he decided to take a stand and assert his authority come what may, including reprisal by the Twins and Doña Manuela.

Having come to a major decision, Captain Montes wrote a letter which was delivered on the 19th, to the Duke of Alvercorre, who had been appointed Governor-at-large of all outlying districts by Viceroy Cortés. In the letter he fully apprised the Duke of the situation that had been created by Doña Manuela

JOSÉ VALDEZ

and asked for reinforcements to cope with a situation that was becoming explosive. By advising the Duke well in advance he was helping his superior arrive at an equitable decision before the documentation accusing Doña Manuela reached his office. Also, having done this, he was helping his own status with the Duke, hoping that Doña Manuela would not find out the contents of the letter before the verdict was pronounced.

Early in the afternoon of the 22nd, Doña Manuela's spy came to announce that the two brothers, Don Enrique and Don Ruben, had started on their journey to the Capital, and the Twins immediately sent a rider by another route to advice the contingent of thugs already stationed at the "Venta de San Juan" to be on the lookout for the Bragelone brothers. The news lifted the gang's spirit because in the first place action was better than idleness; and in the second place overcoming the brothers and emptying their well-lined pockets would bring a breath of life to the gang, for a while anyway.

As had been planned by Don Carlos, the Bragelone brothers started first toward the St. John's Inn, and at staggered intervals, Antonio and Daniel Pardo would follow, with Pepe and Luisa bringing up the rear, the idea being not to attract undue attention. Don Enrique and Don Ruben were going to spend the night at the Inn, and they would start on their way to the Capital the next day, the 23rd of December which would be the last official working day of the year, as all offices were going to be closed beginning with the 24th until the Feast of Epiphany, January 6th. All were riding at a steady pace, and as they neared the Inn, around dusk, they redoubled their vigilance for they knew that Doña Manuela's henchmen would no doubt make their appearance soon.

72

Pepe Makes A Startling Discovery

While bringing up the rear, Pepe and Luisa would have liked to talk with each other, but all they could do was ride close to one another and touch hands every once in a while because they did not want to attract undue attention for no one could be sure that along the way, protected by the lush forest, some of the Twins' villains could be hiding behind some of the massive trees along the trail.

The dull rhythmic sound of the horses' hooves and his own monotonous movement brought about the horses' gait sent by Pepe into a sort of reverie which unconsciously, as if he were completely detached from the Pepe of the past twenty years, reviewed for him the various steps that had brought him to

JOSÉ VALDEZ

his present state. He saw that even at a tender age he could not understand why there was a difference in the endeavors of his people and that of the Spaniards. His people worked hard and he did not see any Spaniard working up much sweat on any given job. Then his wandering mind brought the question closer to home when he started comparing his father to Don Carlos, his mother and Doña Virginia and finally, he, himself, had learned that there was a limit to is schooling for a number of reasons: the law did not allow him to continue his education either because there were no funds to defray the extra expense or, as it was pointed to him once before, he had attained the age and build necessary to join the men of the encomienda in the everyday labors assigned by the Spaniard supervisors. Why such a discrepancy? Was it the color of the skin? Or was it because they were the conquerors?

Every time he tried to rationalize on these factors he seemed to stop short of an acceptable reason. Why, if any of those factors were true, he asked himself, was he sitting on such a lofty position? And what about the others that were beginning to better their situations, like for instance Antonio, the stable boy, who more and more endeared himself to Don Carlos who singled him out not only because he could train and take care of horses better then anyone, indian or Spaniard, but because Don Carlos saw in Antonio a young man of many talents; and even now there he was, a few yards in front, having been selected to accompany the brothers?

Also, in the years past his boyhood, Pepe had come across many Indians who were born leaders, and the supervisors, recognizing their ability, allowed them to run the assignments by themselves. This resulted in a better relationship between the two sectors because on one side the Indians enjoyed a measure of freedom working at their own pace, and on the other side the overseers and supervisors also had an easier time. Actually, in some instances there was laughter and fun and in time a measure of rapport was established. All of these things Pepe stored in his mind, for having the position of mayorazgo of the family of Don Carlos, at some time in the future and perhaps sooner than he expected, he would have to meet head on all the problems of the encomienda, as Don Carlos had attained the ripe old age of fifty-eight years.

All in all, he concluded, given the same advantages and under the same circumstances anyone could reach the same goals. It was here that his mind showed him the burning desire to attain equality with the white Spaniard. He remembered instances when he had told himself that he had made strides in his quest for equality - Don Carlos wanted him close in the hacienda because he had, unwittingly, discovered that Luis was in reality a female and Don Carlos decided that the only way to keep the family's secret was to keep Pepe close to the hacienda. Later, he was made a supervisor mainly on the strength of his association with Luis, when they; sparred with Don Carlos' swords. Then came the episode of the encounter with the Twins, Teodoro and Doroteo, which in his mind he classified as a very important step in his search for equality.

It was a long and difficult process of evaluation and soul searching that finally made Pepe realize that what he had been pursuing was a delusion, a fantasy, for equality was not to be found in riches, family clothes and titles, or special speech that tried to hide the real meaning of one's thoughts; but in the person's make-up, and his or her mental and moral values.

JOSÉ VALDEZ

Now he began to understand more about the way of life that had been thrust upon him and his race and he intended to do something about it for now he was sure he understood that the equality he had sought had always been there. Of course there had to be a difference but they were all materialistic. The gods of his ancestors had not bothered to classify anybody. It was a simple matter, a sort of law of the strongest. But now comes this new God who always insisted that all had been created equal and that all had a right to better themselves. No wonder Pepe had always wondered what he would do if he ever acquired the equality he had been looking for, for it had been there all the time.

At that moment Pepe felt at peace with himself and in his mind he thanked his new God for making him see His tenet about all being created equal. A feeling of exhilaration enveloped him and he thanked Him for all gifts received including the lady at his side that had been such an influential factor in his life.

He was shaken rudely from his reverie by the noise of the clash of steel some fifty yards ahead as the trail doglegged to the right. Pepe and Luisa spurred their horses toward the place of action.

73

Six Are Better Than Twelve

Espying the light that was shining through one of the windows of the Inn, Antonio and Daniel spurred their horses to catch up with the Brothers; and it was a good thing that they had made this decision for they arrived in time to see a group of men, roughly about twelve jump from behind trees alongside the trail, circling and attacking the Brothers Bragelone. Don Ruben and Don Enrique immediately dismounted, hit their horses with the flat edge of their swords to get them out of the way and prepared to defend themselves against what looked to be insurmountable odds.

The arrival of Antonio and Daniel brought some relief as about seven of the malefactors turned on them because one of

JOSÉ VALDEZ

the brigands recognized Daniel and shouted, "Let us dispatch the traitor Daniel and his indian friend." Antonio and Daniel, after chasing their horses away, met the group head on, Daniel with his sword and Antonio with his machete. The spirit of his ancestors took hold of Antonio who began brandishing his terrible machete like a man possessed, while Daniel was doing the same with his sword because he knew that his former companions wanted nothing less than to take his life.

The Brothers Bragelone fought like they had never fought before for there seemed to be no escaped, but they felt a little confidence when they disposed of two of their attackers, one of which was not for this world anymore. Knowing that the rest of the gang would be coming their way, they withdrew toward one of the wider trees for protection against the attack from the rear and held their ground. Out of the corner of their eyes against the moonlight, they saw Antonio and Daniel doing the same thing for protection from being attacked from the rear.

Daniel was never one of the best swordsmen, but in this case his strength and maneuvers were superb, as one of the attackers could have testified had he been able to do so. Daniel had no fear anymore, and he could have fought even the Master of Arms himself if the Master of Arms had been a member of the gang. Antonio, in the meantime, whirling his machete in all directions, found the blade of one of the brigands and neatly cut it in two parts. The impetus blow of Antonio deviated his machete that came to rest on the shoulder of his unarmed attacker who fell lifeless to the ground.

In a matter of two or three minutes, Pepe and Luisa arrived at the scene, dismounted, chased their horses away and cut a swath through the group of outlaws in order to be on the side of Antonio and Daniel who would have fallen notwithstanding their courage and daring because of the overwhelming odds for there were still five against two. Pepe and Luisa lost no time in asserting their superiority and at a very opportune time, for Antonio and Daniel seemed to be flagging. Pepe engaged one of the malefactors who looked like a worthy opponent, while Luisa engaged two or more. Antonio and Daniel took on one apiece with renewed vigor, encouraged by the presence of Luisa and Pepe.

Of the two attackers that Luisa confronted, one gave up completely when she disarmed him by running her sword through his upper right arm leaving his arm bleeding profusely and inert. At this time and with things well in hand because Pepe had also taken his adversary, Luisa told Pepe, "My uncles need help." Pepe ran to the place where the Brothers were fighting three of the gang and with his help two more thugs were past medical aid, and the other yielded.

Completing the rout, Luisa disabled her opponent, Daniel's adversary gave up to his former companion, but Antonio's machete claimed another victim, for as he explained afterward, it is very difficult to recall a stroke of machete once it is on the way. Don Enrique, faithful to his humanitarian principles attended to all that needed assistance, including his brother and Daniel Pardo. The only one who seemed to have a charmed life was Antonio because the attackers had a healthy respect for the machete and tried to fight the indian from quite a safe distance.

JOSÉ VALDEZ

It is to be noted that of the five which set upon the Brothers, the one who yielded, who happened to be 'Calvo' (baldy), ran into the woods and grabbing one of the horsed rode back at breakneck speed to give the Twins and their sister the bad news of the operation. After the rest of the outlaws who could still walk were secured, and the wounded taken care of by Don Enrique, Don Ruben, Antonio and Daniel found lodging at the Inn as the Brothers with Daniel and Antonio accompanying them were going to the Capital to discharge their duties. Pepe and Luisa headed back herding the members of the gang who were still alive to La Morada and to turn their prisoners over to Captain Montes, who immediately put them away in cells that seemed to have been waiting for worthy occupants.

74

Doña Manuela And The Twins
Play Their Last Card

Early that same afternoon, back at the hacienda an attack by the Twins was being launched because they had mistakenly assumed that Pepe and Luisa were going to be overcome by their henchmen at the Inn, or at least were going to be too busy to be able to return to La Morada and by that time they, the Twins, would have accomplished their vengeance on Don Carlos by making shambles of his proud hacienda.

The Twins, as was done previously in All Soul's Day, jumped over the Watergate and started to make their way to the veranda where they expected to find Don Carlos and Doña Virginia enjoying the cool of the evening in solace and comfort. However, as the Twins later found out to their

• 256   JOSÉ VALDEZ chagrin, they did not expect Don Felipe to be with Don Carlos and his wife. The reason that Don Felipe was at the hacienda at this hour was that of late, Don Felipe had formed a habit of visiting his cousin and his wife every afternoon and evening in his craving for company, as his wife had deserted him and his son had embraced a religious life.

The massive panels of the door leading to the spacious chamber that served many purposes such as fiestas, celebrations and games were open and to close them required quite a bit of force. As all three sat outside the chamber, when close to dusk, they espied a group approaching from the Watergate and they immediately surmised that they were going to be set upon, obviously by the Twins and cohorts.

Instantly, Don Carlos rushed inside and took form the wall his best sword, and Doña Virginia did the same, while Don Felipe took out his weapon and stood ready for action. Even though Don Carlos kept begging Doña Virginia not to place herself in danger for it was his responsibility to take care of his wife and home, in this case, she did not obey him for she knew that her sword was going to be needed.

The attackers, some eight of the, including the Twins leading the charge, head to circle the pond, which in a way turned out to be somewhat of an advantage because all the attackers could not spread out because the area between the pond, its adjoining brick walk and the right panel of the massive door which opened to the outside, offered Don Carlos, Don Felipe and Doña Virginia an opportunity to deal with only three or at the most, four of the attackers before the other four could manage to close the door panel that was obstructing their intent to enter the fray.

After dusk had settled and the assault had begun the Twins were puzzled to see before them another person of good stature, instead of only Don Carlos and Doña Virginia, whom they expected to be dealt with quickly. This last assumption as was expected was not going to happen because Doña Virginia, being in her prime, had previously demonstrated her prowess and valor when on All Souls Day she had engaged and disabled one of the brothers known as from the Terrible Trio. In the first charge Don Felipe ran his sword through one of the attackers who mortally wounded, but in return, he received a terrible gash across his left shoulder from another member of the gang and started weakening but was still contending in acceptable form with the one that had wounded him. Doña Virginia and Don Carlos engaged each Teodoro and his twin brother, Doroteo. This last one was quite sure that it was Don Carlos he was fighting and directed his taunt to him, "Don Carlos, it is pay time, and I am here to collect." Don Carlos would have liked to answer but it seemed to be a waste of breath, and besides he did not want to betray himself by showing that he was becoming winded. A couple of minutes later Don Carlos was wounded in his left arm although Doroteo did not appreciate the damage he had done.

While Don Felipe took on his remaining adversary and Doña Virginia was still engaging Teodoro, Don Carlos told Don Felipe, "They are closing the panel. Let us withdraw inside before they close it." By that time the noise had already alarmed four or five servants who risking their lives dragged Don Carlos who had stumbled; and Doña Virginia, even though she had her hands full, with a quick lunge dropped

Doroteo who was bent on killing the prostrate Don Carlos thereby carelessly leaving himself wide open. Doroteo fell bleeding profusely from a deep stap on his side, and Doña Virginia kept withdrawing to the inside of the chamber while redoubling her efforts to protect the servants who were assisting Don Carlos. About that time, Don Felipe, while getting weaker, managed to dispose of his other adversary and helped distract Teodoro while Doña Virginia tried to engage the other four thugs and both Don Felipe and Doña Virginia made their way inside and latched the door before turning their attention to give first aid to Don Felipe and Don Carlos. Knowing that the wounds of her husband and his cousin required professional medical attention, she told one of the servants to go find Doctor Alberto Mendez and bring him immediately.

Teodoro would not be denied. He and two of his men found tree branches that had been destined for the fires in the kitchen, and started using them as battering rams on one side window trying to break the heavy shutters of the left side window, while the other two thugs were doing the same on the right side of the window. The servants also prepared for the assault by arming themselves with whatever could be used as weapons. In their midst was Juana, who having met death twice before was, to coin a phrase, champing at the bit.

In the meantime, Calvo had arrived at the Twins residence to give them the news of the St. John's Inn disaster, but finding nobody at home, guessed what was probably taking place at the hacienda, where he headed right away. Pepe and Luisa, who were some fifteen to twenty minutes behind Calvo, finally found Captain Montes and discharged their onerous cargo that were put in jail forthwith. While performing his duty, Captain Montes advised Pepe and Luisa that since it was believed by all concerned that they were staying at the Inn overnight, and would return on the next day, the Twins might take advantage to try to do some damage at the hacienda. Captain Montes did not have time to finish his advice because Luisa and Pepe were already galloping at a furious pace toward the hacienda.

75

Doña Manuela And The Twins
Can't Win For Losing

Doña Virginia and Don Carlos, who had recovered sufficiently, stood together inside the left window waiting for the onslaught as soon as the window panels were broken by Teodoro and two of his gang, while tow more thugs worked on the panels of the right side window. Don Carlos assigned the servants to the right side window while Juana tended to Don Felipe's serious wound. The left side window started to give and Don Carlos and Doña Virginia stood ready to bet their lives that Teodoro would not enter.

When banging at the front door, accompanied by calls from someone call her name were faintly heard by Juana, notwithstanding the din going on, she could not believe her ears, and thanking the Lord for whoever were at the door who might lend a hand to help, she fairly flew to the front door, and seeing Pepe and Luisa, between sobs and incoherent speech managed to tell them enough of what was happening on the other side of the mansion. In a couple of seconds Pepe and Luisa reached the chamber and embraced Doña Virginia and Don Carlos, and heard a voice well know to them holler in glee, "We have it now, men, and you will be well rewarded."

All recognized the voice of Teodoro, and Pepe advised Don Carlos, "Please, father, go to the right side window where the servants need your presence and your courage because this miserable excuse of a human being is mine; and it is high time he got paid for all his vile and dastardly deeds." Don Carlos replied, "Be careful, son, for it is in a situation like this that a hyena is most dangerous and will even fight a lion.." Don Carlos then added, "Come, Virginia, and let us welcome the other henchmen at the other window." While following her husband, Doña Virginia gave Pepe and Luisa one more piece of advice, "Give a good account of yourselves, children, for the Lord is on our side." Outside the right window, the banging grew a little stronger because there were now three thugs as Calvo had also jumped the water gate fence in order to take part in the attack.

The shutters of the windows had been opened from the inside in order to facilitate action against the intruders, and also to prevent further useless damage. When one of the outside panels of the left window gave way allowing enough room for an assilant to enter, one of the thugs who tried to jump inside sword in hand, fell mortally wounded across the base of the window when Luisa ran him through as he got ready to jump to attack her. The other panel gave way, too, and Teodoro pulled outside the mortally wounded assailant; and recognizing Pepe and Luisa, shouted, "I did not expect you, miserable Indian, so now my revenge will be doubly sweet because I am going to send you where your blood thirsty ancestors are waiting for you."

While the right window was still resisting the battering of the other three assailants, Teodoro and his companion engaged, respectfully, Pepe and Luisa. Lardon, who engaged Luisa, and who was known as one of the brothers known famous as the 'Terrible Trio,' between invectives, directed a derisive taunt at Luisa, "So you are the famous 'La Morada'; well, little girl, I have more than one bone to pick with you. First of all, my companions think you are something out of this world but I am going to prove otherwise. Also, my brother Tamon received a terrible wound on All Souls Day from your mother who took advantage of the terrain, and I am here, also, to avenge him." Luisa, after a few thrusts and lunges figured Lardon's style of play and knew that she could finish her adversary whenever she wanted, and said, "Señor Lardon, your motives may be received, understood and perhaps lauded by people of your ilk; but to me, you are only a vulgar individual, with a very coarse knowledge of sword handling, and if you don't stop insulting remarks and persist in trying to cross swords with me, I will be forced to cut you into little pieces. My advice to you, therefore, is to yield before something drastic happens to you."

Lardon did not take Luisa's advice and by chance and in a very careless maneuver on the part of Luisa, touched her on her right upper arm which did not bother Luisa much but started the blood oozing out of her slight gash. Thinking that perhaps the affected muscle might shrink or contract, Luisa decided to end the uneven contest and stop Lardon's mocking and scoffing because he had seen the bleeding arm, and changed her sword from her right arm to her left. Upon seeing this, Lardon stood confused and dumbfounded at Luisa's strange tactic and could not stop Luisa's thrust to his abdomen causing Lardon to fall in a heap of bleeding profusely, while she ran to her parent's side as the panels started to give way on the right side.

In the meantime, Pepe directed to Teodoro some well chosen remarks that perhaps showed to Teodoro that he was not the blood thirsty indian that Teodoro was accusing him of being, "Señor Teodoro, before you go to your ancestors, something you richly deserve, I want you to know that ever since I was four years old I started looking for you because I saw you kill my father by stabbing him in the back, a cowardly act. Although I did not see your face, I saw the red markings on your boots, and I have no doubt whatsoever that you killed my father, like a coward, through his back."

Teodoro replied, "It won't do you a bit of good, indian, because I am going to send you to where he is so that you can have a reunion." At this, Pepe remembered Don Carlos' advice and did not lose his temper but became mechanical and very methodical in his tactics did not even try to take advantage of lapses by Teodoro. Pepe tested Teodoro's strength from time to time and noticed a little difference every time, and that told him that even if his adversary did not realize it, a battle of attrition was in progress. Teodoro spent a great amount of energy using the heavy logs as battering ram against the outside panels of the left window, and it was only a matter of time that his strength would desert him. Pepe bided his time and when Teodoro, in one last desperated effort tried to lunge at Pepe, he became impaled in Pepe's sword and fell to the floor mortally wouded, while imploring for someone to bring him a priest to hear his confession.

Upon seeing what had befallen their leader, the last three assailants, who had finally battered the panels of the right side window, yielded when they saw Don Carlos, Doña Virginia, Luisa, Pepe, Captain Montes and Juana with a host of servants armed to the teeth confronting them. Captain Montes had arrived a few minutes before because he had guessed what was taking place at the hacienda, and when the last three attackers yielded, he took them into custody and on the spot wrote a lenghy report with the deposition of all that were able to do do.

Doctor Mendez and his most able assistant, Juana, had their hands full tending to Don Felipe, Doroteo, Lardon and Luisa, who only had a small scratch on her right arm; while Father Damien was hearing Teodoro's confession who was truly sorry he had wasted his life in shady endeavors, and hoped his brother Doroteo and his sister, Doña Manuela, would mend their ways.

76

All's Well That Ends Well

Very early on the 23ʳᵈ, the Brothers Bragelone accompanied by Antonio and Daniel Pardo, who insisted that his wound not prevent him from riding, set out for the Capital to contact the offices of the Duke of Alvercorre in order to file all the documentation concerning the accusation of Doña Manuela by Don Carlos. The audience with the Duke did not last long because the Duke already knew the details of the case from the letter that he had received from Captain Montes a few days before. The official verdict was given right on the spot, and due to the fact that a member of the aristocracy was involved in the case, the Duke made use of his extraordinary powers by holding the sentence in abeyance for a period of two years, which period Doña Manuela would have to spend in a contact and with no content whatsoever with the outside world. After the period of two years, the sentence would either be meted or canceled.

The reason for this leniency that was exhibited by the Duke was to preven undue embarrassment to the Aristocracy that could have ugly repercussions among the lower classes. After rendering his decision, the Duke ordered the captain on duty at the time to travel immediately to La Morada to bring Doña Manuela to be interned in the convent of the Dominican Sisters; and also, to bring all her follwers, including her brothers, which heretofore had been known as the Twins. All of these orders were accomplished by the squad of men sent for the purpose, although it was not the easiest undertaking the squad of soldiers had ever gone through because as the saying dictates, 'There is no fury like that of a woman scorned.'

With the removal of Doroteo on a stretcher and Doña Manuela in a well protected coach, the complete obliteration of the wayward element in La Morada was accomplishment, and on the first day of the long period of festivity celebrating the Birth of our Lord, the 24th of December, Don Carlos requested that Father Bermudez and Father Damien concelebrate a High Mass to give thanks to our Lord and his Virgin Mother for her intercession in bringing peace and happiness to the community.

To top if all, during the High Mass Pepe received the Holy Sacrament of Confirmation that made him a full member of the Church, his sponsors being Don Enrique and Don Ruben. Present at the ceremony and in place of honor were Juana, his mother, Don Carlos and his wife, Doña Virginia, Luisa, Don Felipe, Don Marco di Georgio, the Master of Arms, Captain Montes, who had appointed Provost Marshall by the Duke because of his timing and duty, and all the servants and members of the encomienda, leaving the hacienda as there was no danger of any incursions.

After the ceremony, there were congratulations and felicitations all around, and plans were held in abeyance to elect a mayor, and offcials needed to represtn the community on official contact and correspondence with the Captial because La Morada was growing and Progressing. To this effect Don Enrique's proposal that Don Ruben serve in that capacity because of his legal background, until proper election be held, was accepted by acclamation.

One last item deserving mention, at last report, Felipe Jr., by his demeanor, hard work and dedication earned the respect and praise of his superiors, who predicted a bright future for him, while Luisa and Pepe, duly sanctioned by everybody enjoyed a tender passion for each other which made Don Carlos and Doña Virginia very happy.

The afternoon was dedicated by everyone to make all preparations necessary for this last posada of the Christmas Season to be the best ever as peace, contentment, happiness and prosperity once more reigned throughout La Morada.

THE END

EPILOGUE

After the Christmas Season came to a close on January 6th, Epiphany being the reenacting of the Adoration of the Infant Jesus by the Magi, on which day in some countries the children leave their shoes outside for the Magi to put gifts in them, the citizenry of la Morada had practically forgotten the events that had done away with the wayward faction that had terrorized the settlement. One last function was performed in a central place which had been designated as public grounds for erecting a sort of plaza, and that was to publicly give a vote of thanks to Don Carlos, Doña Virginia, Don Felipe, Luisa, Pepe and even Juana and all others that had taken part in the eradication of the malevolent crowd.

Don Carlos, known for his largesse, gave Antonio and Pardo generous gifts and new assignments for their valor.

Captain Montes acquired stature and well-deserved respect, and thanked his stars for guiding him to choose the honest but sometimes very difficult and dangerous road.

Luisa and Pepe continued their courtship even though their position was fraught with what at first sight were considered anomalies – sister and brother in love, with full acquiescence of Don Carlos, Doña Virginia and Juana.

Everything was fine and everybody was looking forward to a very happy and prosperous year, except for Don Carlos, Don Felipe and Captain Montes who held private conversations about the future because the concensus was that the indomitable Doña Manuela would find ways to escape from the nunnery, and as far as Doroteo was concerned since he was now the head of the family and in possession of the wealth that had been accumulated, he was sure to find a way to either escape or have his sentence shortened or commuted by a judge receptive to a considerable bribe. At any rate, a plan of action was contemplated for the future, which would take care of such a disagreeable event.

JOSÉ VALDEZ

CLARIFICATION OF SOME POINTS

Note 1 : It is with a slight regret that the quantity of dialogue is now what some readers and/or critics might expect, but a couple of episodes in the story will make up for this deficiency by capturing their attention, especially when the young heroine wins a fencing tournament by switching her weapon to her left hand just when it seems that she was going down to defeat.

Note 2 : As can be seen by the table of contents, it appears as though there is a repetition of names, and in some cases, abreviation of, citing an example, PEPITO and PITO, but that is not the case as those are the names of different characters.

Note 3: Lady Virginia married Don Carlos and by a freak accident Doña Virginia fell while walking to a horse's stall, and when Doctor Bragelone was called, his announcement was made that Doña Virginia could not have any more children. Also, as a result of the accident LUISA eventually became LUIS and she was brought up as a male. Since only the oldest male child may become 'Mayorazgo", the duplicity was kept through the years, and even LUISA (now LUIS) learned about the deception when she became of age. She did not mind this too much because from an early age her yearning was to be and act like a boy, and she was accepted as such because being athletically inclined, she was good enough to compete with any boy her age. Doña Manuela, looking forward to her husband inheriting everything, did her best to find out exactly what Mother Nature had done in the baby's constitution, but Juana, who knew all about the deception evasively kept the baby from her.

Note 4: At the time of this story the governments of Spain and what was known as New Spain had enacted laws that were quite tolerant about transgressing women than what the change that evolved, say some 250 years later when some countries' laws changed; so when Doña Manuela was sentenced to spend her life in a convent, that was hardly the punishment of a lady of her sinful conduct. It is to be imagined that with her bag of tricks and evil mind no convent could hold her. By breaking out Doña Manuela would go underground, reorganize her followers and begin dealing misery, perhaps in a sequel?

JOSÉ VALDEZ